PRAISE FOR THE WALKER PAPERS

URBAN SHAMAN

"A swift pace, a good mystery, a likeable protagonist, magic, danger—*Urban Shaman* has them in spades."
—Jim Butcher, bestselling author of *The Dresden Files*

THUNDERBIRD FALLS

"Thoroughly entertaining from start to finish."
— Charles de Lint

COYOTE DREAMS

"Tightly written and paced...a compelling, interesting protagonist, who...will captivate new & old readers alike."
—Romantic Times Book Reviews

CAULDRON BORNE

"Another gripping, well-written tale."
—RT Book Reviews

DEMON HUNTS

"Murphy has the ability to weave mythology with a strong, likeable protagonist...hard to put down."
—Amber Benson, actor & author of *Death's Daughter*

SPIRIT DANCES

"Readers will be thrilled... Fast-paced, repartee is fantastic, the magic is exciting."
—Publishers Weekly

RAVEN CALLS
"The twists and turns will have readers...devouring the
page."
—USA TODAY

MOUNTAIN ECHOES
"...the penultimate chapter of Murphy's outstanding and
long-running series...[an] emotionally charged novel."
—RT Book Reviews

SHAMAN RISES
"An epic end to an epic series...a perfect conclusion."
—Fangs for the Memories

ALSO BY C. E. MURPHY

THE WALKER PAPERS

Urban Shaman * Banshee Cries * Thunderbird Falls * Coyote Dreams * Cauldron Borne *
Demon Hunts * Spirit Dances * Raven Calls * No Dominion * Mountain Echoes * Shaman
Rises

THE OLD RACES UNIVERSE

Heart of Stone * House of Cards * Hands of Flame * Baba Yaga's Daughter * Year of
Miracles * Kiss of Angels

THE WORLDWALKER DUOLOGY

Truthseeker * Wayfinder

THE GUILDMASTER SAGA

Seamaster * Stonemaster * Skymaster * Sunmaster * Witchmaster

THE STRONGBOX CHRONICLES

The Cardinal Rule * The Firebird Deception * The Phoenix Law

THE HEARTSTRIKE UNIVERSE

Atlantis Fallen * Coming to America * From Coffin to Grave

THE BORDER KINGDOM

Roses in Amber * Wintergate

THE INHERITORS' CYCLE

The Queen's Bastard * The Pretender's Crown

MKP

BANSHEE CRIES

Print ISBN: 978-1-83557-002-9

E-Book ISBN: 978-1-83557-003-6

This edition contains the exact same story as the original book did, unmodified save for extremely minor details like the author changing a few sentences so the print edition would be prettier.

Cover Art & Design: G&S Cover Design Studio

Cover Model: Marissa Turcotte

BANSHEE CRIES

BOOK TWO: THE WALKER PAPERS

C.E. MURPHY

*This one's for my mom, Rosie Murphy,
who wanted to know what the story
with **Jo's** mom was*

AUTHOR'S NOTE

Banshee Cries was originally published in the anthology *Winter Moon* as 'Book 1.5' of the Walker Papers. With the reissuing of the series, it has been promoted to a full Book Two status, and the numbering of the books going forward will reflect that.

Aside from the numbering, there are no changes from the original release of *Banshee Cries* to this one.

CHAPTER I

Cell phones are the most detestable objects on the face of the earth. Worse than those ocean-variety pill bugs that grow bigger than your head, which were on my personal top ten list of Things To Avoid.

My life had been a lovely, cell-free zone until nine weeks, six days, and four hours ago. Not that I was counting. On that fateful day I got an official business phone to go with my bulletproof vest and billy stick. I'd even been given a gun to go with my shiny new badge.

I wanted those things about as much as I'd wanted to bonk my head on the engine block I'd sat up beneath when the phone rang. I rubbed my forehead and glared at the engine, then felt horribly guilty. It wasn't Petite's fault I'd hurt myself, and she'd been through enough lately that she didn't need me scowling on top of it all.

The phone kept ringing. I rolled out from under the Mustang and crawled to her open door, digging the phone out from under the driver's seat. "What?"

Only one person outside of work had the phone number. As soon as I spoke I realized that a politer pickup might have been kosher. The resounding silence from the other end of the line confirmed my suspicion. Eventually a male voice said, "Walker?"

I turned around to hook my arm over the bottom of the car's door frame and did my best to stifle a groan. "Captain."

"I need you—"

These were words that another woman might be pleased to hear from Captain Michael Morrison of the Seattle Police Department. Then again, if he was saying them to another woman, there probably wouldn't have been the slight tension in his voice that suggested his mouth was pressed into a thin line and his nostrils flared with irritation at having the conversation. He had a good voice, nice and low. I imagined it could carry reassuring softness, the kind that would calm a scared kid. Unfortunately, the only softness I ever heard in it was the kind that said, *This is the calm before the storm,* which happened to be how he sounded right now. I crushed my eyes closed, face wrinkling up, and prodded the bump on my forehead.

"—to come in to work."

"It's my weekend, Morrison." As if this would make any difference. I could hear his ears turning red.

"I wouldn't be calling you in—"

"Yeah." I bit the word off and wrapped my hand around the bottom of Petite's frame. "What's going on?"

Silence. "I'd rather not tell you."

"Jesus, Morrison." I straightened up, feeling the blood return to the line across my back where I'd been leaning on the car. "Is anybody dead? Is Billy okay?"

"Holliday's fine. Can you get over to Woodland Park?"

"Yeah, I—" I tilted my head back, looking at the Mustang's roof. Truth was, I'd been futzing around under the engine block because I couldn't stand to look at the damage done to my baby's roof anymore. A twenty-nine-inch gash, not that I'd measured or anything, ran from the windshield's top edge almost all the way to the back window. From my vantage, thin stuffing and fabric on the inside ceiling shredded and dangled like a teddy bear who'd seen better days. Beyond that, soldered edges of steel, not yet sanded down, looked like somebody'd dragged an ax through it.

Which was precisely what had happened.

A little knot of agony tied itself around my heart and squeezed, just like it did every time I looked at my poor car. The war wounds were almost three months old and killing me, but the insurance company was dragging its feet. Full coverage *did* cover acts of God—or in my case, acts of gods—but I'd only said she'd been hit by vandals, because who would believe the truth? In the meantime, I'd already spent my meager savings replacing the gas tank that somebody'd shot an arrow through.

My life had gotten unpleasantly weird in the past few months.

I forced myself to find something else to look at—the opposite garage wall had a calendar with a mostly naked woman on it, which was sort of an improvement—and sighed. "Yeah," I said again, into the phone. "I'm gonna have to take a cab."

"Fine. Just get here. North entrance. Wear boots." Morrison hung up and I threw the phone over my shoulder into the car again. Then I said a word nice girls shouldn't and scrambled after the phone, propping myself in the bucket seat with one leg out the door. Bedraggled as she was, just sitting in Petite made me feel better. I patted her steering wheel and murmured a reassurance to her as I dialed the phone. A voice that had smoked too many cigarettes answered and I grinned, sliding down in Petite's leather seat.

"Still working?"

"Y'know, in my day, when somebody made a phone call, they said hello and gave their name before anything else."

"Gary, in your day they didn't have telephones. Are you still working?"

"Depends. Is this the crazy broad who hires cabbies to drive her to crime scenes?"

I snorted a laugh. "Yeah."

"Is she gonna cook me dinner if I'm still workin'?"

"Sure," I said brightly. "I'll whip you up the best microwave dinner you ever had."

"Okay. I want one of them chicken fettuccine ones. Where you at?"

"Chelsea's Garage."

Gary groaned, a rumble that came all the way from his toes and reverberated in my ear. "You still over there mooning over that car, Jo?"

"I am not mooning!" I was mooning. "She needs work."

"You need money. And snow tires. And more than six inches of clearance. You ain't gonna drive it till spring, Jo, even if you do get it fixed up."

"Her," I said, sounding like a petulant child. "Petite's a *her*, not an *it*, aren't you, baby," I added, addressing the last part to the steering wheel. "Look, are you gonna come get me or not? It's even a paying gig. Morrison called and wants me to go over to Woodland Park."

"Arright." Gary's voice brightened considerably. "Maybe there'll be a body."

. . .

MORRISON GLARED MAGNIFICENTLY when I arrived with Gary in tow. The two of them facing off was wonderful to behold: Morrison was pushing forty and good-looking in a super-hero-going-to-seed way, with graying hair and sharp blue eyes. Gary, at seventy-three, had Hemingway wrinkles and a Connery build that made him look dependable and solid instead of old, and his grey eyes were every bit as sharp as Morrison's. For a few seconds I thought they might start butting heads.

But Morrison pointed at Gary and barked, "You stay here." Gary looked as crestfallen as a wet kitten. I actually said, "Aw, c'mon, Morrison," and got his glare turned on me. Oops.

"It's arright, Jo." Gary gave me a sly look that from a man a few decades younger would've had my heart doing flip-flops. "I bet there's a body. You can tell me about it at dinner. You need a ride home?"

"I'll take care of it," Morrison said in a sharp voice. Gary winked at me, shoved his hands in his pockets, and saun-tered back to his cab, whistling. I choked on a laugh and turned to follow Morrison, tromping through a truly unbe-lievable amount of snow. It had started snowing in mid-January and, as far as Seattle was concerned, hadn't stopped in the two months since. Even the weathermen merely looked stunned and resigned, mumbling excuses about hurricane patterns in the South having unexpected consequences in the Pacific Northwest.

"What is it with you two?"

"So what's going on, Captain?" We spoke at the same time, leaving me blinking at Morrison's shoulders and starting to grin. "What *is* it with us? Me and Gary? Are you serious?"

"He answers your phone." Morrison was talking to the

footprints in the snow in front of him, not me. My grin got noticeably bigger.

"Only the once. That was like six weeks ago, Morrison. And who told you that, anyway?" I wanted to laugh.

"I'm just saying he's a little old for you, isn't he?" Morrison's shoulders were hunched, as if he was trying to warm his ears up with them. I grinned openly at his back and lowered my voice so it only just barely carried over the squeak and crunch of snow as we walked through it.

"All I'll say is, you know how they say old dogs can't learn new tricks? Turns out old dogs have some pretty good tricks of their own."

Morrison's shoulders jerked another inch higher and I laughed out loud, the sound bouncing off tree branches black with winter cold. Snow shimmered and fell off one, making a soft puff and a dent in the snow below it. Morrison flinched at the sound, head snapping toward it as his hand dropped to his belt, like he'd pull a weapon. My laughter drained away and I followed him the rest of the way to a park baseball diamond in silence.

He climbed up snow-covered bleachers, making distinct footprints in the already walked on snow, compacting it further. I put my feet in precisely the same places he'd stepped, fitting my sole print to his exactly. We had the same size feet, and in police-issue boots his prints were indistinguishable from mine, at least to the naked eye. A forensics officer could probably tell there was a weight difference between the two of us—in Morrison's favor, thank God—but for the moment I enjoyed the idea of stealing along behind the captain, invisible to anybody trying to track me.

Morrison stopped on the step above me and turned so abruptly I nearly walked into him. I rocked back on my heels, one step below him, my nose at his chest height as I frowned up at him. "Thanks for the warning." I hated looking up, physically, to Morrison: we were the same height, down to the half inch that put us both just below six feet, and any situation that made me look up to him made me uncomfortable.

Of course, the reverse was also true, and I'd been known to wear heels just so I'd be taller than he was. No one said I was a good person.

"Tell me what you see."

Assuming he didn't want me to describe him—which, had he not been so antsy about the snow falling from the tree a few moments ago, I'd have probably done just to annoy him—I turned away, looking over the baseball diamond.

It was buried beneath two feet of the wet, heavy snow that had made my jeans damp from tromping through it. I shook one foot absently, knocking snow off my boot. I'd lived in Wisconsin for a winter, so snow wasn't entirely new to me, but this was ridiculous for Seattle, and I said so. Morrison huffed out a breath like an annoyed bull and I puffed my cheeks, muttering, "Okay, fine. I see snow."

Well, duh. Clearly Morrison wanted more than that. "Snowmobile tracks. I didn't even know people in Seattle owned snowmobiles. Um. Footprints around the diamond, like people've been playing snowball." I thought that was pretty clever. Snowball, like baseball, only with snow, right? Morrison didn't laugh. I sighed. Poor, poor put-upon me.

"There are cops, there's some teenagers over there, there's—" Actually, there were a lot of cops, now that I was looking. Picked out in dull blue under the grey sky, they worked their way around the baseball diamond and stumped their way through the outfield. "There's, um." I frowned. "I don't hear anything, either. There aren't any people around. Dead trees..."

"No," Morrison growled, full of so much tension that I looked over my shoulder at him, feeling my expression turning worried. "What do you *see*," he repeated, and suddenly I got it. A drop of ice formed inside my throat and spilled down into my stomach, like drinking cold water on an empty belly. I folded my arms around myself defensively, shaking my head.

"Shit, Morrison, it doesn't—it doesn't work like that. I mean, I'm not, like, good enough to make it work, I don't know how, I don't *want* to—"

"God damn it, Walker, what do you *see*!"

I turned back to the field, stiff as an automaton, my lower lip sucked between my teeth. One of my arms unfolded from around me completely of its own will, hand drifting to rub my sternum through my winter jacket.

There was no hole in my breastbone, no scar to suggest there'd ever been one. But I found myself pulling in a very deep breath, trying to rid myself of the memory of a silver blade shoved through my lung and the bubbling, coppery taste of blood at the back of my throat. I'd nearly died eleven weeks ago, and instead found that buried within me was the power to heal myself, and maybe a great deal more. More than one person had called me a shaman since then. I didn't like it at all.

"I'm not any good at this, Morrison. I don't know if I can do it on purpose." My voice was strained and thin, full of reluctance. Morrison didn't say anything. Once upon a time—not that long ago—the only thing he and I had had in common was a complete disdain for the paranormal and people who believed there were things that went bump in the night. I'd been struggling for the past three months to get back to that place. Back to a world that made sense, where I didn't feel a coil of bright power burbling in the core of me, waiting to be used. I desperately wanted to believe it had been some kind of peculiar dream. Most days I was able to cling to that.

Morrison was not helping me cling. I could feel the tension in him, not with any extrasensory perception, but with how still he was holding himself, and the deliberate steadiness of his breathing. He wasn't any happier than I was about asking, which perversely made me willing to play ball. I put my teeth together, muttering, "Only you could get me to do this."

That struck me as being alarmingly accurate. I found myself abruptly eager to do it, so I didn't have to think about what I'd just said.

Unfortunately, I was at a complete loss as to how to proceed. I'd pulled denial over my head like a blanket the past several weeks. Now that someone was asking me to use my impossible new gifts, I didn't know where to start.

Just thinking about it made the power inside me flutter like a new life, full of hope and possibility. I swallowed against nausea that was as unpleasantly familiar as the idea of life inside me, and tentatively reached for the bubble of power.

A spirit guide called Coyote had suggested to me I work through the medium I knew best: cars. In reaching for that bubble of energy, I tried to do that. Morrison wanted me to *see*. Well, if I wasn't seeing clearly, then the windshields needed washing.

Power spurted up through me, a sudden warm wash that felt startling against the cold winter afternoon. A silver-blue spray swished over my vision, just like wiper fluid. I closed my eyes against the brightness and a perceived sting and, without really meaning to, envisioned windshield wipers swooping the liquid away, leaving my vision clear. The sting faded and I opened my eyes again.

The world was beautiful. Even the grey sky glimmered with light, sparks of water shimmering above me. As I brought my gaze down, trees whose branches were weighted with snow flickered with the greenness of waiting life, only cold and dead to the mundane eye. Sap waited to rise, leaves prepared to bud, all a promise of explosive activity the moment winter let go its hold. The chain-link fences that surrounded the ball field had their own resolute purpose, created and placed to do a specific thing. A distinct sensation of pride in doing the job emanated from them.

The people on the field radiated different energy, swirling colors that bespoke worry or fear or determina-tion, the rough shapes of their personalities hammering into me and leaving nothing taken for granted. I wanted to turn and look at Morrison, to get a sense of him with this other sight I'd called up, but I was afraid if I moved, I'd lose it again. I dropped my gaze to the field itself, still not knowing what I was looking for—

And a wave of maliciousness slammed into me like a tornado. It whipped around the core of power inside me and dug claws in, sharp knife-edges of pain cramping my belly. It sucked the heat out of me, draining the coil of energy in sudden throbs, faster than a heartbeat. My knees crumpled, light-headedness sweeping over me.

Morrison caught me under the arms so easily he might have been waiting for me to fall. I twisted toward him, grabbing his coat as he slid an arm around me more firmly.

"You're all right." His voice sounded like it was coming

from unreasonably far away, given that I knew he was right behind my ear. "I've got you."

I didn't want to move, desperately glad for the support he offered, both physical and other. His presence was solid and comforting, a wall of commitment and strength in deep, reassuring purples and blues. I doubted he knew he was projecting his own personal energy in a way that let me borrow some, but I was incredibly grateful for it.

I managed a shaky nod, hanging on to the flow of strength he offered, using it to shore up my own depleted silvers and blues. After a few seconds I was able to get my legs under me again, though Morrison didn't quite let me go. I locked my knees and made myself turn to look at the field again.

Crimson lines, bleeding with pain and rage, flowed up from the field, following the lines of the baseball diamond. Points of vicious black stabbed behind my eyes, making marks that seemed to shoot up into the sky and fade somewhere beyond the stars. Looking at the field felt like someone was digging talons into my innards, trying to pull them out and bind me to the death that had already been wrought there.

Gary was wrong. There wasn't a body.

There were three.

CHAPTER 2

"C 'mon, Walker. Tell me what you see. Talk to me, Walker."

"How many have you found?" My voice was groggy, as if I was talking through pea soup. Morrison let out a breath that sounded like it meant to be a curse.

"Just the one. What're we missing?"

"Two more." I slid out of his grasp and to the snow-covered bleachers. My jacket wasn't nearly long enough for sitting on, and cold started seeping through my jeans immediately. "All women. There and there and there." I pointed blindly at the field, unable to convince myself to lift my eyes and study it again. Not that it would've helped: the snow was only snow again, not breathing with its own chaotic pattern of lights. I was just as glad that I couldn't hang on to the second sight for long. "What the hell made you call me in for this?"

"Holliday."

That explained a lot. Billy Holliday—besides having one of the more unfortunate names I'd ever encountered—was the department's number-one Believer. I'd played a mocking Scully to his Mulder until my own sensible world turned upside down. He'd been remarkably kind, all things considered, in not giving me too much shit since then. If something struck him as genuinely abnormal about the murders, it made a certain amount of sense for him to think of me.

God, how I wished he hadn't. I slumped down, forehead against my knees, which reminded me that I'd smacked my head earlier. I pressed my palm against it, trying—not very hard—to call up just enough of that energy inside me to smooth the bump away. It didn't work. I was almost grateful. It suggested I wasn't as completely weird as the past couple of minutes proved me to be. My silence drew on long enough to prompt my boss to keep talking, something I hadn't intended but for which I was also grateful.

"Some teenagers found the first body. Holliday was on call and when they dug her free—you should probably see for yourself."

"Do I have to?" My voice was still thin. "I'm a beat cop, Morrison, not a homicide detective." I'd never wanted to be either, despite having attended the academy. I'd been a mechanic, and the short version was Morrison'd hired my replacement when I had to go overseas for a while. But thanks to my mixed ethnic heritage—I'm half Cherokee—I looked too good on the roster to actually fire. Instead, I'd gotten an upgrade from mechanic to actual living breathing cop. Morrison figured—hoped—I'd spit in his face and quit.

I couldn't stand to give him the satisfaction. Which left me sitting in the snow, whining and praying he'd give me a break.

"You have to."

So much for praying. I got up, brushed snow off my cold bottom, and stumped down the bleachers.

BILLY'D OBVIOUSLY BEEN on duty when the kids called in about the body, because he was wearing sensible shoes. Typically, when he got called unexpectedly he came in wearing a pair of great heels, which I still noticed because he had better taste in shoes than I did. I'd never heard anybody tease him about cross-dressing, partly because he was a hell of a detective, and partly because he was something over six feet tall and looked like he could break you in half. It didn't hurt that his wife could've been Salma Hayek's slightly more gorgeous sister. At the moment, though, he was wearing regulation boots and crouched over a frozen woman whose insides were no longer in. I stopped several feet back and said, "Jesus," by way of announcing my arrival.

The woman's intestines stretched out of her belly and into the snow, ropy frozen lines of blackness buried in the cold. Her stomach had been cut open in an efficient X, and judging from the rictus her face was frozen in, she'd probably been alive when it happened. If it'd been summertime, I probably would have lost my lunch, but the icy strands and beads of cold on her face looked so surreal I couldn't quite wrap my mind around it having been a person once. She looked like a prop on a sound stage for a movie set in the Arctic.

"Hey, Joanie." Billy was watching the guys from forensics brush snow away from the woman's body, careful detailed work that gave lie to the fact that the weather had almost certainly destroyed any available evidence. "Glad you could make it." He pursed his lips and shrugged. "Well."

"I know what you mean." I edged a few steps closer, staring down at the woman reluctantly. "Why'd you want me?"

"Look at her." He shrugged again. "Got ritual murder all over it."

"Did the dead lady tell you that?"

Billy gave me a dirty look that I deserved. I'd only learned recently that some of his intuitive leaps in homicide cases were courtesy of an occasional ability to converse with ghosts. It was not the kind of thing I was comfortable with, even though—or particularly because—I could now do it myself. "No," he said. "The physical evidence did. Can you not make jokes right now, Joanie? This woman deserves some respect."

"These women." I let out a long exhalation, looking at my feet. "There's two more. I...saw them."

Satisfaction showed in Billy's voice for just an instant. "I knew bringing you in was the right thing to do. You get anything else?"

Creepy-crawlies shivered over my skin, making me even more uncomfortable than a wet butt and dead bodies did by themselves. Billy was much, much easier with weird shit than I was. The shamanic gift that I hated having would have been far better off residing in him. "No. I'm sorry." I forbore to mention I didn't have a clue *how* to get anything else. He looked disappointed enough as it was. I lowered my voice, feeling like a member of a Sekrit Brotherhood that dared not voice its name. "Did you get anything?"

Billy shook his head. "Been dead too long. I never get anything from people who've been dead more than forty-eight hours. They lose their connection with the world."

I nodded, then frowned. "I thought you said your sister visited you three years after she died."

"I guess blood's thicker than ether."

The wind picked up as he spoke, a hair-raising keen that had no business anywhere outside of a holler. I instinctively lifted my shoulders against it, then felt a scowl crinkling my forehead so hard it ached. There was no new chill in the air, no cutting cold through my coat, despite the shriek of sound. A shadow came down over the world, making me look up at the sky, as if the sun wasn't already hidden beneath doomfully grey clouds.

There were no clouds. A window framed the section of sky I could see, scattered stars valiantly struggling against the light of a brilliantly full moon. Irish lace curtains caught at the moon's edges, making it whimsical and delicate in the clear black sky. Seattle's snowbound chill was driven from my skin, and the breath I took was full of warm air and the scent of tea.

Recognition jolted through me like needles under my fingernails. I knew the window; I knew the curtains, and I knew that if I looked to my left I would see a near stranger, lying beneath a handmade quilt and dying of nothing more than her own determination to do so.

I turned my head, for all that I didn't want to look at the woman on the bed. She had black hair, worn much longer than mine. It lay in soft-looking waves against her white pillow, stark contrast in the moonlight. Even in the blue-white light, her eyes were very green, and her skin was nearly as pale as the pillowcase. I heard myself say, "Mirror, mirror, on the wall," which I certainly hadn't said in real life. I wouldn't have let myself, even if I'd dared.

I was a wildly imperfect reflection of the woman on the bed. Where her skin was uniformly smooth and pale, mine was marked with a handful of freckles scattered across my nose; where her features were fine, mine seemed too sharp or too blunt. She was tall, although not as tall as I was, and had a degree of elegance to her that my long limbs and mechanic's hands could never emulate.

Her skin changed color, a horrid sallowness creeping in. I looked back at the moon to see blood draining over it. Fear scampered through me, the pure childish terror of the unknown. My voice broke as I said, "Sheila?" but when I turned to her, the woman was gone.

"Joanie?" Billy's hand on my elbow, big and warm, brought me back to the field with a start. I looked at his hand, then up at his worried frown. "You all right?"

"Yeah. I just...kind of spaced out. Sorry. I don't know what that was. Did you say something?" The wet chill of Seattle winter settled back into my bones, leaving me scowling at nothing. The moon had been full the night my mother died, but we hadn't spoken. We hadn't had much to say to one another, not from the time she'd called me out of the blue to say she was dying and she'd like to meet the daughter she abandoned twenty-six years earlier. I'd gone out of a mixed sense of duty and curiosity, and spent four uncomfortable months that culminated in her death on the winter solstice, almost three months ago to the day.

"I said, do you think there's anything else you can pick up? You've got more mojo than I do." His grin suggested he was biting his tongue to not ride me harder than that.

"I'll, um...shit." The last word wasn't meant to be heard, but Billy laughed anyway. I curled a lip and waved it off, perversely glad that he was teasing me a little. "I'll try." I wanted to try about as much as I wanted to stick red-hot pokers against my feet, but I couldn't quite bring myself to say that to the one person who didn't think I was at all crazy.

Granted, he was nuts himself by any normal standards, but I wasn't in a position to be throwing stones. "Is the morning soon enough?"

Billy turned a sad smile on the woman's body, then made a gesture to encompass the rest of the field. "There's a lot to do here, and I don't think another night is going to make this any harder on anybody. You work tomorrow?"

"Yeah. I'll give you anything I've got before I go out on patrol." I admired the weary confidence in my voice, as if I actually expected to come up with anything.

The problem was that I was afraid I might.

"All right. Thanks, Joanie." Billy hesitated a moment before adding, "I know you don't like this."

"So I'm a great sport for going along with it. I know. Tomorrow, Billy."

It was more than not liking it. It was like fingernails on chalkboards combined with dentist drills on unnumbed teeth. My world was a sensible, straightforward place. Checking out ritual murders on a psychic level simply did not belong. I kicked clumps of snow as I slogged back to Morrison to bum a ride home. He was driving his personal vehicle, a gold Toyota Avalon XLS—which I thought of as the American version of "boxy, but safe!"—so he hadn't been on duty when he'd called me. I didn't envy him his job.

Neither of us spoke during the whole drive, both wrapped up in our individual discomfort of what I was doing there. I didn't even say thanks when I got out, just thumped the top of his car and watched him drive off. Only after he disappeared down the Ave did I go into my building, taking the steps up to my fifth-floor apartment two at a time.

Gary, to whom I was practically certain I had not given a key, was hanging out in my apartment playing Tetris on my computer. "Thought you never touched the things," I said as I unlaced my boots.

"You didn't leave any entertainment rags. What was I supposed to do?"

"Cook dinner?" I put the boots on the carpet where all the melting snow would be absorbed and slid into the kitchen in my stocking feet.

"Nothin' to cook. I looked."

"Details, details. Besides, there is, too. I've got at least three different frozen dinners in here." I heard the telltale musical bloop that said he'd died horribly in the game, and a moment later he appeared in the door frame, making it look ridiculously small with his bulk. Even in his eighth decade he retained the build of the linebacker he'd once been, a fact that he took no small amount of pride in.

"So. Was there a body?"

I pulled two microwave dinners out of the freezer. "Do you remember calling *me* a bloodhound when we first met?"

"Nope." Gary gave me a disarming smile. "So there was a body."

"There were three. And..." I really didn't want to say anything else. I busied myself stabbing holes in the plastic tops of the dinners, then mumbled, as fast as I could, "And I said I'd maybe do a little checking out of what was going on in the astral realm sort of thing I don't suppose you'd hang around and bang a drum after dinner."

"Eh?" Gary cupped a hand behind his ear, leaning forward a little and wearing a cocky grin that would do

James Garner's Maverick proud. "What'd you say? I'm an old man, lady. Can't hear when you don't speak up."

"I hate you, Gary."

He beamed at me. "Now, that's no way to talk to an old man, Joanne Walkingstick."

"Augh! Gary! No! Stop that!" I'd dropped my last name along with the rest of my Cherokee heritage when I gradu- ated from high school, and a compulsive slip of the tongue —was there such a thing? It had felt like it at the time—had caused me to mention the long-since-abandoned name to Gary the day we'd met. "It's Walker. Don't do that, Gary." The humor I'd started with fell away into discomfort and I shrugged my shoulders unhappily as I put the first meal into the microwave. "Please."

"Hey." He came into the kitchen to put a hand on my shoulder and turn me around. "No harm meant, Jo. You arright?"

"I just..." I summarized the experience at the park, staring alternately at his feet and my own, not wanting to meet his eyes. "I just hate this shit. And the thing with remembering my mother all of a sudden just freaked me out." The microwave beeped and I turned back to it, my stomach grumbling. Gary put a hand on the door, keeping me from opening it.

"Let's hit the voodoo stuff first, darlin'. Food grounds you, you know that. You're shooting yourself in the foot by eating first." He lifted a bushy eyebrow. "Or is that on purpose?"

I squirmed, feeling like I'd been caught being naughty. Gary grinned, bright flash of white teeth that looked like he'd never smoked a cigarette in his life, and steered me into the living room. "Where's your drum?"

"Bedroom." I dragged a cushion off the couch and

stuffed it against the front door, cutting off the draft that circled from beneath it. Gary went into my bedroom like he belonged there and got my drum.

It was the only thing I owned of any intrinsic value. It'd been a gift from one of the elders out in Qualla Boundary, not long after my father and I moved back there. It was painted with a raven whose wings sheltered a wolf and a rattlesnake, and had a drumstick with a soft rabbit-fur end dyed raspberry red, and a knotted leather end that made sharp rich pangs of sound against the taut leather. Even fourteen years after having been gifted with it, I was still amazed anyone would make something like it for me. Gary knew it, and carried it as if it was fragile, a gesture that made my nose sting with embarrassing emotion.

I settled down on the floor as he came out of the bedroom with the drum and a closed fist. "I thought you might want this."

I turned my hand up and he dropped a silver choker into my palm. Made of tube links intersected by triskelions, it had an Irish cross—a simple quartered circle, identical to the Cherokee power circle—as its pendant. "What—?"

"Your mom gave it to you, didn't she?"

"Yeah, I..." She'd given it to me the day she died. I'd worn it for two weeks, gradually getting used to the peculiar feeling of having something resting in the hollow of my throat, until the day I'd been stabbed through the lung and the necklace had been blackened with my blood. It'd taken days to get the stains out, and I hadn't brought myself to put it back on in the intervening weeks. "Yeah, all right." I swallowed nervously and fastened the choker with fingers that suddenly felt thick and clumsy. "You're all Mr. Insightful tonight, aren't you?"

Gary sat down on the couch cushion that hadn't been scavenged, grinning. "Somebody's gotta be. You ready?"

I nodded, fighting the urge to curl my fingers around the necklace and pull it away from my throat to alleviate the alien pressure of jewelry against my skin. "I'll wake up thirty seconds after you stop drumming." We'd only done this a few times, but establishing the time felt like ritual. Gary started knocking out a heartbeat rhythm, and I let my eyes drift shut, waiting to follow the sound of the drum out of my own body.

CHAPTER 3

I had a deep dark secret. The world I saw through shamanic eyes—the one in which every thing on earth, be it animal, mineral or vegetable, sparked with the essence of life—was a world I dreamed about even when I was dead set against its reality. The world I saw with my spirit eyes was one where I could see Gary's big rumbly presence like a V-8 engine that a girl could rely on. It was one where I could slide through the ceiling and get an alarming look at my neighbors' sexual proclivities—although this time I went through the window when I separated from my body, because I *can* be taught, and I really didn't need another eyeful of somebody else's sex life.

Except for the glimpse that afternoon, I hadn't looked at the world from a spirit's perspective since January, when my life got turned upside down in the first place. There was something off-kilter as I slid into the Seattle night. Winter had come on too hard, and the life in the city that sped below me felt strained, like the world was being pushed in a direction it wasn't prepared to go in. The blues I'd seen a few months ago seemed darker, the electricity of life dammed up in some way. Streets seemed more congested, as if their purpose had been forgotten. It hadn't been like this a few months ago, and the feel of it made my skin prickle. There was a lingering feeling of familiarity below the wrongness, but when I reached for it, it slipped away.

I spun through the air, weightless and silent, watching sudden flashes of red and orange erupt in backed-up traffic, countered by calm waves of blue that I tried to encourage, clumsily. I passed a stretch of road where a woman's astrally projected spirit hovered above her car, looking down at traffic much like I did. Pure boredom emanated from her, as if driving home had been so dull it'd flung her out of her own body. She didn't seem to sense my presence, and I whisked past her, not knowing how to stop and say hello.

I left the city behind without having a destination in mind, moving as fast as thought itself. Color, vivid and strong, streaked with the coldness of winter, shot past me, sometimes forming into recognizable images, but more often staying abstract. I wondered if the abstraction was due to my lack of direction, but with the thought came a clear pathway that I recognized with a startled shiver.

A bower of trees arched over a single-track path, white flowers all but glowing under a source of light I couldn't pinpoint. The path was smooth, as if it had been often walked on. I tumbled from flight to run along it, great huge strides so I felt I was still flying. There was a presence in front of me, somewhere buried in the depths of the earth. It carried its own weight, its own gravity well, drawing me toward it. I careened around a corner, pretending I was driving Petite, and came up against a cave, its mouth blocked off with boulders.

The presence beyond the cave mouth had a genial feeling to it, as if it were amused at my audacity and youth.

I hated feeling like people were laughing at me. I glowered at the boulders and reached for the smallest stone I could find, trying to wriggle it out of its lodged position in the ranks of larger stones.

A vise clamp fastened itself around my wrist, hauled me back, and did something that put my feet over my head and my head against the ground. I lay on my face with a mouthful of dirt, not entirely sure how I'd gotten there but pretty certain that any moment now I was going to start to hurt.

"And what is it," a woman's voice above me asked, "that you think you're doing, Siobhán Walkingstick?" The lilt of Ireland was strong in her voice, almost masking the sarcasm with which the question was delivered.

I was pretty sure she didn't want an answer. I had comparatively little experience with mothers, but the tone suggested to me that she knew perfectly well *what* I was doing, and that the real question was why was I doing something she obviously regarded as unbelievably stupid.

The physical pain I was expecting didn't seem to be coming, so I rolled onto my back and stared up at her. She looked remarkably tall from this vantage, and somewhat bustier than I thought of her as being. She also wore an expression of exasperation that was both more vivid than any expression I could remember seeing on her in life, and which, although strictly speaking was entirely new to me, I had felt on my own face any number of times. Distress settled over me. It didn't seem fair that I was turning into my mother when I'd barely even known the woman.

Eventually one of the numerous things crowding my mind and vying to be said won out: "I asked you not to call me that." It seemed, even at the moment, an awfully calm response to the appearance of a woman I believed to be dead.

I was treated to a second new expression: dismay, which was wiped out almost instantly by the thoughtful, examining gaze that was all I'd really ever seen of her. "Very well, then. Joanne." Her tone spoke volumes about what she thought of my Anglicized name, but I was almost entirely overwhelmed with not caring. I got to my feet somewhat stiffly, although I suspected any injuries I'd sustained were in my own mind.

Of course they were. That's what happens when you travel on the astral plane. Moving on, then. I looked back to the wall of rocks, eyeing the one I'd initially grabbed. "Joanne," my mother said in a remarkably good "don't you dare test my patience one more time, young lady" voice. I dropped my hand and turned to face her, making a point of looking around rather dramatically.

"I'm sorry," I said. "Did you think you had something to say to me that I might listen to? Is there some burning reason that I should pay attention to, I don't know, what are you, a banshee or something? You're dead, Mother. We didn't much like each other when you weren't dead. Why don't we just leave it at that and you can go do whatever it is dead people do? I'm busy."

"Busy."

"Yes." I went to work on my rock again, tugging it a few millimeters out of the wall. She clamped her hand around my wrist again. Her fingers were tremendously cold, not just like the dead, but as if she was emitting cold the way a living body emits heat.

"You don't understand what you're doing, Joanne." I hated the warm lilt of her voice, a low alto that I wanted to instinctively trust. I couldn't possibly have recognized it. She'd abandoned me with my father when I was three months old, but from the moment she'd called me, seven months ago, I'd fought against wanting to curl up in the warmth and safety of that voice and letting myself forget about the world.

"Like you could possibly know what I'm doing. I don't even know what you're doing here. Go *away*." I yanked my wrist, trying to escape her grasp. I failed in that, but I did manage to loosen the rock I held. The entire wall shifted ominously, deep scrapes of stone bumping down a few inches against one another. My mother hissed, a sound like an angry cat, then lifted her voice in a high keen that made me jerk away again, this time succeeding and clamping my hands over my ears.

"You will not pass this barrier, Siobhán Walkingstick." Her voice thundered inside my head, making me equal parts angry and dizzy. I set my teeth together and stomped forward, grabbing my stone again.

They always say, "I never knew what hit me." Technically, I knew what hit me: it was my mother. Beyond that, I really don't know what happened, except one second I had the stone in my hands and the next I was about forty feet away, lying on my back in the dirt, and she was standing over me like one of God's avenging angels in a blouse and long skirt. My lip was bleeding. I lifted the back of my hand to it, staring up at her. She crouched, putting a hand on my shoulder. It seemed to carry the weight of the world behind it, as profoundly heavy as the draw that had pulled me toward the cave mouth in the first place.

"You are not yet ready to face what lies beyond that wall, daughter. I haven't much time to act, and less time still to tell you about it. Get yourself home. I've no energy for wasting on sullen little girls who refuse to listen to their mothers."

Her will hit me like a wall itself, reaching right for the core of energy inside me as if it was her own. She shoved me into the earth with the hand on my shoulder, using my own stored power as her focus point.

I popped out the other side and into my body so hard I fell over backward. Gary stopped drumming and jumped to his feet while I stared at the ceiling and tried to determine if all my parts were where I thought they should be. They were. After a few seconds I said, "Ow," and thought I'd leave it at that.

There was no part of me that didn't hurt. It wasn't the god-awful pain of having a sword driven through me, but I ached, like someone had...well, shoved me through solid ground. I said, "Ow," again, for good measure, and pushed myself up slowly. Gary hovered over me, nervous but kind enough not to ask.

"What the hell happened?"

All right, kind enough not to ask for a few seconds, at least. I shook my head, exhaustion sweeping over me without warning. The bubble of energy inside me that I spent so much time trying to ignore was depleted again. I felt like I'd been depending on it without knowing about it. "I need food."

I got up, largely to see if I could, and wobbled to the kitchen door. When I'd reached the frame without mishap, I turned my head to answer Gary's question. "I don't think my mother is as dead as I thought she was."

I refused to say anything else until I'd eaten. Gary finally stopped asking, "Zombie? Vampire? Wraith?" and ate his own dinner, watching me with the eagerness of a kid at Christmastime. I swear, anybody on the planet—except possibly Morrison—would have been better suited to my insane new world than I was. Billy had already lived with something like it his whole life. Gary thought it was cool. I wanted it to all go away so I could sleep in peace at night, and work on Petite by day.

"There's something out there," I finally said. Gary gave an evocative snort that made me aim a kick at him under the table. To both our surprise, it connected, and he yelped, looking injured.

"Sorry. I mean, something that wants me to go check it out. My mother was standing sentinel over it tonight. She wasn't there last time."

"Last time?"

"I saw it in January. Look, that doesn't matter. She kicked my ass."

Gary put a bite of spaghetti—the closest thing I had in the freezer to chicken fettuccine—in his mouth to hide a smirk. I drew my foot back for another kick, then remembered I'd managed to hit him once already and felt guilty. He looked smug, making me annoyed for feeling guilty, so I swung at him again. I missed. "So obviously," I said through gritted teeth, "she thinks whatever's behind door number one is dangerous."

"Then you should stay away from it," Gary said wisely.

"I don't even know what it is!"

"Mothers are always right. Don't you know that?" He wrinkled his eyes into nonexistence as I scowled at him. "Right. I forgot. Sorry." He paused. "Mothers are always right. You don't wanna find out what's behind that door."

"Gary!"

He lifted his hands defensively. "I'm just sayin'."

"Well, dammit, I want to know what's back there." I hesitated. "She said I wasn't ready for it."

Gary's bushy eyebrows rose. "If you'll excuse me for coppin' a phrase from today, *duh*. You really think you're ready for the monster in the closet?"

"No, but I'd like to know what it is! Knowledge is half the battle, or something."

"Look." Gary pointed his fork at me. "What'd you go in there looking for?"

I shrugged, uncomfortable. "I don't know. Nothing specific."

"Okay. There's your problem. You got no focus. You need to go in there and talk to somebody who knows what's going on. Your buddy the coyote."

"Coyote never gives me a straight answer." I sounded just like the sullen kid my mother had accused me of being.

"Yeah, that's kinda what the whole trickster thing is all about, Jo."

I flung my hands in the air. "Why do you know that? Why does everybody on the whole planet know this stuff that I don't? Why didn't somebody else get this stupid talent? You can have it. You'd be a lot better at it than I am!"

Gary huffed. "Probably."

My rant cut off as my jaw dropped. Gary's grey eyes sparked good humor with a steely undercut. "You done?"

"Uh." I cleared my throat. "Um. Yes. Thank you."

"You got something special, kid. You're gonna have to learn to suck it up and live with it, or walk away. Right now there's some dead ladies out there that maybe you can help, if you stop your whining and bitching and get on with it. Are you gonna do that, or what?"

"Okay." I sounded very small and pathetic. And embarrassed.

"Arright." Gary got up, his plastic spaghetti dish in one hand. "Let's go try this again, then." He stalked into the living room, leaving his muttered, "Jeez. Dames," lingering on the air.

IT TOOK LONGER to go under this time, in part because of chagrin and in part because of the microwaved fried chicken that settled in my tummy and made me more aware of my body than was helpful. After several minutes of drumming, though, I suddenly fell backward into my body and found myself scrambling down a thin tunnel, in search of an internal garden that somehow reflected the state of my soul.

There was a fundamental difference between going there and going...other places...that I went. It struck me that it might really be helpful to get a grasp of the different levels of reality that I seemed to be able to access. Being able to name them, for example, could be useful. It might make me sound—or at least feel—like less of an idiot.

Whether I had a name for it or not, the journey to my garden felt distinctly internal, whereas moving to the astral plane seemed to involve leaving my body in some kind of upward fashion. I scuttled through little tunnels, feeling myself drawing closer to the center of me, until the light turned grey around me and I popped out of a mouse-sized hole in one of the walls surrounding my garden. I looked back and the hole was gone, sealed up safely by my meager mental defenses.

The garden itself was—well, it wasn't quite dead, which was something. It was functional, not beautiful, with straight pathways in geometric patterns and grass cropped so short I could see dirt between individual blades. A small pond with its own waterfall bubbled at one end of the garden, more agitated than I remembered it being. I took a couple of deep breaths to see if it would calm the pond, but it didn't seem to help.

"The problem's deeper than your breathing, Joanne."

"I don't have any problems!" There I went again with the juvenile-response syndrome. I waited a few seconds, trying not to blush, then looked for the speaker, who lolled on a concrete bench, his tongue hanging out. I tried very, very hard to modulate my voice into politeness as I said, "Hello, Coyote."

He rolled to a sitting position and shook himself all over, golden eyes bright as he cocked his head at me. "If you don't have any problems, what are you doing shouting for me?"

"I—" I took a deep breath and stood up straighter. "I need some, um, help. Guidance!" I latched on to the word, feeling rather proud of myself. "Please," I added hastily. "If you could." *Nice Mr. Coyote Man,* I thought but didn't say. I didn't have to: he snapped his teeth at me like I was an annoying fly.

"I heard that."

My shoulders sagged. Coyote could hear anything I thought, while I heard nothing of what he thought. Sometimes I thought that meant I'd made him up. Other times I was equally certain it meant I hadn't.

"You did not make me up," Coyote said.

"No," I muttered. "You'd be cuter and less annoying if I had."

He grinned a coyote grin at me and stretched, long and lazy. When he was done stretching, he wasn't a brown and gold beast any longer. Instead an Indian man sat there, his skin as red as bricks and his hair blue-black and long and falling to his hips. He wore jeans and was barefoot, looking incredibly comfortable in his own skin. Only the eyes were the same, bright gold and full of mirth. "Is this better?"

It was certainly cuter. He laughed even though I hadn't spoken out loud, and stood up to go drag a hand through the bubbling pool at the end of my garden. "What do you need, Jo?"

"There've been some murders. And...my mother is alive. Or something. I—can you help me find her?"

He lifted his head in a swift motion, more like a coyote than a man. "Your mother?"

"Is up there in the astral realm or whatever it is, bossing me around."

"Wow."

I was practically certain spirit guides were not supposed to say *wow*. "Cause you know so much about spirit guides," he said. "I'll see if I can—"

"You won't be needing to, lad."

"Jesus Christ!" I whipped around, unbalancing myself with the motion, to find my mother standing directly in front of the mouse hole that I could've sworn closed up when I arrived. She ignored me momentarily, focused on Coyote.

"Sheila MacNamarra," she said to him. "A pleasure, and aren't you the handsome one. Joanne's a lucky girl."

My dead mother was matchmaking me with a dog. Great.

"I'm not a dog."

"I'm hardly matchmaking, Joanne. You opened up the conduit. I'm just here to say hello."

I set my teeth together and waited a few seconds before I trusted my voice. "Hello, Mother." I waited a few more seconds before it burst out of me: "What the hell are you doing alive?"

A trace of surprise and injury darkened her eyes. "I'm not alive, Joanne. You saw me die."

"Then what are you doing here? Besides kicking my ass back into my body, which hurt, thankyouverymuch."

"Not nearly so much as facing down that enemy would have hurt. Joanne—" Sheila made a small and elegant gesture, bringing her hands in toward her heart, as if collecting sorrow there. "There's very little time, and a great deal to tell you. I'd hoped we could talk before, but you weren't ready—"

"Before what?"

"Before I died," Sheila said, nonplussed. "That was why I asked you to come, of course. I never dreamed you'd be so closed off. If you'd been ready, I could have explained so much."

"Ready for *what?*" I felt very small and young suddenly, a feeling that was reflected in the garden: it grew around me dramatically, until Coyote and my mother both towered over me, and even the sparse blades of grass seemed much larger in comparison to my own height.

My mother cast a glance at Coyote that clearly said she despaired of me, but she brought her attention back to me in an instant. "To accept your heritage, at least on my side. What you've got to face. You're still not ready to hear it, but the moon is changing and I'm out of time. Siobhán, listen to me. I'm a *gwyld,* a—"

"Shaman," I interrupted dully. I'd heard the word before, only directed at me, not my mother. "Some kind of druidic version of a shaman. You came back from the dead to tell me *that?* Like it could possibly matter? Like I could care?" I was not, I knew, being fair. Part of me did care. Part of me cared so much it hurt to breathe, and that was the part that lashed out at her. It was perversely like finding out there was a Santa after all.

Frustration creased her forehead. "I left the mortal world to protect you, Siobhán. I've known since before you were born what you might be, what it was you'd have to face. But you were so unprepared I saw no other choice. You needed protecting."

"What," I said, "if you strike me down I'll become more powerful than you can ever imagine? Is that your gig?"

Complete incomprehension flitted across her expression. I set my teeth together, about to lash out again, but a shriek of wind erupted, sounding in my ears but going unfelt against my skin. My gaze went to the sky even as a shadow, dark and red, fell across my vision again. A full moon hung above me, one that hadn't been shining on my garden moments before. One with blood spilling down its face, and with a piece of darkness falling from it like a scythe. A deep sense of malignancy boiled up inside me, as if a thing of hatred was being born. Cold, raging hands seemed to clench around my heart, and I listened frantically for the rhythmic drumbeat that would let me know I was still alive.

My mother let go an inhuman screech, like a car braking too hard, and flung herself at the sky. Her hair spread out like raven's wings, blocking my view of the bloody moon. The slice of night that had fallen from it was enveloped by the black spiderweb of her hair. I heard another yowl, as gut-wrenching as the earlier ones, and the barbs that had knotted in my heart loosened.

A small, furry bundle of bone crashed into my chest, knocking my heart into pounding again as sweat stood out on my body in cold terror. Coyote stood over me for a moment or two, his golden gaze fixed on mine before he brought his head down to smash it against mine with tremendous force.

For the second time in a single evening, I slammed out of the realm of Other and back into my body, aching all over with pain and confusion.

CHAPTER 4

It took the better part of an hour to get Gary out of my apartment, which both made me feel better and worse. When he was gone I sat on the couch with a pillow hugged against my chest, staring blindly at nothing.

It was inconceivable to me that my mother had been some sort of mystic. The woman I'd known for a few scant months had held her cards close to the chest, always judging and never commenting. I'd spent four months with her and, when she died, felt as though I'd known nothing more about her than she liked Altoids. There'd been no real mourning, at least not on my part. Confusion, yes, and, not to be delicate about it, a whole lot of resentment. She'd disrupted a life in which I had not missed her to any noticeable degree in order to have me witness her death. She'd been young, only fifty-three, and in extremely good health. I'd been left with the impression that she was bored of life, and as such saw fit to leave it under her own power.

It appeared that the power in question was more literal than I'd thought. I mean, anybody who could will herself to death wasn't a person whose emotional state was one I wanted to tangle with. She might decide it was time for me to die, and I might not be tough enough to argue. I hadn't even tried arguing in favor of her life, which probably made me a very bad daughter.

Not that there was any really compelling reason to be a good daughter to the woman who'd abandoned me when I was a few months old. We hadn't liked each other as adults. I could only assume she hadn't much cared for me as a baby, either.

A fine thread of emptiness wove through me, an ache that I'd spent the better part of my life resolutely ignoring. I hadn't been given up for adoption by a mother who thought it was best for me. I'd been dumped on a father who hadn't known I existed until that moment, by a mother who evidently didn't like me very much. It was not something I enjoyed thinking about.

Especially as it reminded me, inevitably, of a boy growing up in North Carolina, whom I had known full well I couldn't properly mother. Not at fifteen. Not in the confusion of mourning the sister who'd been born with him, and who'd died just minutes later, too small to live.

I set my teeth together and put my forehead against the pillow, shoving away every thought of family ties that came haunting me. Introspection was not my strong suit. I didn't like to look back, and I wasn't prepared for the past, in the form of my dead mother, to come calling.

I fell asleep sometime after midnight, still wrapped around the scratchy couch pillow.

MONDAY, MARCH 21, 8:20 A.M.

There was a place on the other side of sleep that I'd been to, where I'd walked among the dead and spoken with them.

The plan—a plan which I didn't have any intention of mentioning aloud, not even to myself—had been to whoosh through dreamtime, find the dead women and learn who'd killed them, then jaunt off to work like Don Juan triumphant.

Instead I woke up stiff and disoriented the next morning, curled up on the solitary couch cushion, without having had a single moment's otherworldly experience while I slept. An ache of uselessness welled up behind my eyes. Not only did I not understand what was going on, but the baser part of me didn't care. Having it all go away would have been far more within my comfort zone.

I had just used the phrase *comfort zone* with all due seriousness, right inside my own head. I clearly needed to get up, stick my head in a bowl of cold water, and drink a pot of strong coffee. Which I did, except it was a hot shower instead of a cold bowl, and I swear I didn't drink more than three cups of coffee. Honest.

I called a cab—not Gary; he knew too much about me and I wasn't up to facing that this morning—and went to work, my nose mashed against the window. I missed Petite. I wanted to be cozy and safe, driving her instead of taking a cab. I had a better relationship with my car than I had with most people.

With any people, a small and somewhat snide voice inside my head said. I told it to go away, paid the cabby, and stumped through the precinct building to find Billy.

Actually, I was looking for his desk, where I figured I could leave a note explaining my humiliating inability to find anything useful, and then run away before I had to confess my failure out loud. I'd come in early just to be sure I could pull that off.

Billy was earlier. He leaned on his elbow, big palm

wrinkling the side of his face until his left eye had all but disappeared into the curves of flesh. He looked like he'd been up all night, which was not only possible, but likely. An attack of guilt grabbed me by the throat. I snuck back out of the precinct building and scurried down the street to the doughnut shop to get him a lemon-poppyseed muffin and an oversize mocha. His face actually lit up when I plopped them down on his desk several minutes later, which made me feel slightly less like a loser.

"You're a goddess." The side of his face was one big red mark from leaning on his hand too long. He unwrapped the muffin, took a slurp of coffee, and squinted up at me. "You didn't get anything about the murders, did you."

"Is it that obvious?" Back to Loserville.

"You look like a kicked puppy. But I'll forgive you anything for the next five minutes, because you brought me the manna of heaven."

"Damn." I looked at the muffin, impressed. "I shoulda gotten me one of those things."

Billy chuckled and sank back in his chair, its un-oiled hinge drawing out a creak that slowly lifted every individual hair from my fingertips to my nape. I wrapped my hands around his coffee cup for a few seconds, trying to chase the chill away. He ate half the muffin in one bite, then nodded at his computer screen, speaking around crumbs. "I'd forgive you anyway. I found some stuff out. Not about our dead girls. They all had ID, by the way. We're seeing if they've got anything in common, but so far they look random. Anyway, the murders."

Somehow I was able to understand every word he said. I usually couldn't understand most of what I said when my mouth was full. I twisted around to look at the computer screen. "Interpol?"

"Thought of it this morning. I remembered reading about some kind of ritual murders about thirty years ago—"

"You read them thirty years ago?" Billy wasn't more than ten years older than I was. He gave me a look that suggested I shut up. I pressed my lips together and widened my eyes, all innocence.

"The murders were about thirty years ago. I read about them a few years ago. Pedant."

"Because you what, read about ritual murders for fun?"

"Joanie," Billy said, annoyed. I lifted my hands in apology and tried to keep quiet. Billy glared at me until he was sure I wasn't going to interrupt again, then continued. "These women all had their intestines stretched out, connecting them with one another."

I suddenly wished I hadn't drunk a lot of acidic coffee for breakfast, and looked around for something neutral to eat. There was nothing handy except Billy's muffin, the second half of which he stuffed in his mouth, clearly suspecting that I was about to raid it. A burp rose up through the soured coffee in my stomach and I clamped my hand over my mouth, tasting coffee-flavored bile. Yuck.

"You've got a soft heart, Joanie." Billy gave me a very tiny smile that did a lot to make me feel better.

"I'm not a homicide detective."

"Mmm. Yeah. Anyway, so I remembered this morning reading about a murder like that over in Europe. It's not the kind of thing the authorities like to noise around."

"No kidding." My stomach was still bubbling with ook. "So we've got a copycat?"

"Either that or somebody's changed his hunting grounds. Anyway, the only case there was an eyewitness for was, like I said, about thirty years ago. A woman who was presumably supposed to be the last victim—there's never more than four—fought back and managed to escape. The Garda Síochána—"

"This was in Ireland?" I didn't mean to interrupt. It just popped out. Billy's ears moved back with surprise.

"Yeah. What, you had some run-ins with the cops while you were there?"

"No, I just remember my mother talking about the Garda. She didn't call them the Síochána." I said the word carefully, *SHE-a-CAWN-a*. "I had to ask her what it meant."

"It means police," Billy said helpfully, then waved off my exasperated raspberry. "Yeah, you know that, right. Anyway, they weren't able to find the guy, and for a while the woman was under suspicion, but she got off when the marks on the victims' bodies had obviously been made by somebody a lot bigger than she was. They're usually strangled into semiconsciousness before the horrible stuff begins."

"Like being half-strangled isn't horrible." It had nothing on having your innards ripped out while you were still alive, and I lifted a hand to stop Billy's protestation. "I know. So what was her name? Maybe we can talk to her, get some kind of information about this psycho that might help us."

Billy leaned forward, chair shrieking protest again, to pull up a minimized screen. "That was my thought. She was from Mayo. I've got some people there looking to see if they can find her. Her name was—oops, wrong window." He pulled up another one, scrolling down. "Her name was—"

"Sheila MacNamarra," I finished, feeling light-headed.

The woman on the computer screen looked more like me than the one I'd known had. There was a ranginess to her that I shared, and our eyes were shaped more alike than

I'd realized. I'd never seen a picture of my mother when she was young, and young she was: the photo showed her from the thighs up. She was obviously several months pregnant.

With me.

I closed my eyes, unable to think while looking at the photograph on the computer screen. "You won't—" I cleared my throat, trying to wash away the break I'd heard in my voice. "You won't find her. She's dead."

"Joanie?" Billy sounded bewildered. "You know this woman?"

"Yeah." I wished I was wearing my glasses so I could pull them off. Instead my hand wandered around my face like a bird looking for a resting space: my fingers pressed against my mouth, then spread out to cover the lower half of my face before curling in again. I couldn't stop the little actions, even when I tried. "She's my mother."

I WANTED the next half hour or so to disappear into a jumble of confusion, but it adamantly refused to. It was all horribly clear, with an overwhelming babble of questions that I caught every syllable of and a host of concerned, confused, angry expressions that wouldn't let me back up and take stock of the situation. No one had known my mother's name, not any more than I knew Billy's mom's name. Everyone had known I'd gone to Ireland to meet her, and that she'd died, but nobody'd pried beyond that, which I'd been perfectly happy about.

Now, though, Morrison was standing over me—well, trying to. I was on my feet, too, unable to stay sitting while he demanded to know how it was I coincidentally had connections to this woman who'd been a suspect, albeit briefly, in a murder case that was nearly thirty years old. He went on for quite a while, during which Billy tried to be the voice of reason and I watched them both with growing incredulity. Finally I edged between them and said, "Captain," which brought Morrison up short. I rarely resorted to using his actual title.

"Look." This was my reasonable voice. I didn't have a lot of hope for it working on Morrison, but I'd never tried it before, and anything was worth trying once. "My mother obviously didn't kill those women. She wasn't big enough. The police reports cover all that. I guess I am big enough." I lifted one of my hands, with its long fingers, and shrugged. "And we have no idea when our women died, so—"

"Actually," Billy said. I winced and looked at him. He grimaced back apologetically and shrugged. "The first body has a fair amount of degradation. They figured she died about three weeks before it started getting cold enough to snow so much, probably around Christmas."

Morrison's cheeks went a dangerous dark florid purple. "You're telling me we had a body lying around Woodland Park for three weeks before it snowed and *nobody noticed?*"

"The good news," I said under his outrage, "is that I was in Ireland at a funeral on Christmas. Good alibi."

"How the hell," Morrison shouted, ignoring me, "did a body lie around in a public park for three weeks without anyone noticing?"

"I don't—" Billy began.

Morrison roared, "Find out!" and stalked into his office, slamming the door behind him. Everyone within forty feet flinched. I sucked my lower lip into my mouth and watched the venetian blinds inside the captain's office swing from the force of the door crashing shut.

"Do you think he does that for dramatic effect?" I didn't realize that was my outside voice until nervous laughter broke around me, then rolled over into outright good humor. Someone smacked me on the shoulder and the audience that had gathered for the drama broke up. It never failed to astonish me how there were always people around to watch tense moments unfold. You'd think none of us had jobs to do.

I followed Billy back to his desk, since I still wasn't on shift for another forty minutes. "I really hate to say this."

He eyed me, wary. "But?"

"But I'm pretty sure nobody was supposed to see that body. I don't think it was cosmic coincidence. I think there was..." My tongue seemed to be swelling up and choking my throat in order to prevent me from continuing my sentence. Part of me wished it would succeed. "Power." *Power* was easier to say than that other word, the five-letter one that began with *m* and ended with *agic*. "Involved."

"Yeah?" Billy's eyebrows rose a fraction of an inch. "Can you do that?"

"Billy, I can't even pick my nose without using a finger." Sometimes my mouth should stop and consult my brain before it says anything. Billy got this wide-eyed look of admiration that belonged on a nine-year-old boy. It said, *Wow, that was really gross*, and, more important, *How come I didn't think of it?* My mouth consulted my brain this time, and I asked, "I don't suppose you could just forget I said that?"

"No," Billy said, in a tone that matched the admiration still in his eyes. "I don't think I can. I'm going to have to tell that one to Robert."

"Melinda will kill you."

Billy's grin turned beatific. "Yeah," he said happily. "Girls don't get stuff like that. Except you," he added hastily. "But you're sort of not like a girl."

I stared at him. After a while he realized he might have said something wrong, and backed up hastily. "I mean, you are—of course, you're a girl, it's just, you know, you're one of the guys."

"Billy," I said. "Bear in mind that what you're saying is coming from a man who wears nail polish. I'm not sure it's helping."

"See, that's what I'm saying. Have you ever worn nail polish?"

"No," I said slowly. "I started to put some on once, but it made my fingers feel heavy and I hated it."

"Okay then. So what I'm saying is I bet more of the guys here have worn fingernail polish than you have."

"So I'm more like a guy than one of the guys." My tone was flat and dangerous. Well, I thought it was. Billy didn't seem to feel threatened.

"Kind of, yeah. You're like an überguy. You know everything about cars and you drink beer and shoot guns, only then you also clean up pretty good—"

"Billy." I was a hundred-percent cranky, and this time he heard it. He looked up, surprise lifting his eyebrows.

"Solve your own damned case." I turned on my heel and stalked away.

CHAPTER 5

I stomped all the way down to the garage beneath the precinct building and peeked around the stairwell wall. Peeking wasn't much in keeping with my stompy mood, but I wanted to see if my archnemesis, Thor the Thunder God, was in the garage before I went in.

He was, of course. I sat down in the shadow at the foot of the stairs—the last flourescent light in the row above the steps had never, to the best of my recollection, been functional—and wrapped my arms around my knees, watching the mechanics at work.

This was where I belonged. I'd gone to the academy because the department had paid my way, but I'd never wanted to be a cop. I was a mechanic and something of a computer geek. The two went hand in hand with modern cars, and I was happy with both labels. But my mother had taken her time dying, they had hired Thor as my replacement, and now I was a cop.

His name wasn't really Thor. It was Ed or Ted or something of that nature. He just looked like Thor, big and blond with muscles on his muscles. He was working on Mark

Rodriguez's car, which was forever having the wheels pulled out of alignment. I had a suspicion that Rodriguez went home and beat the axles with a hammer, but I couldn't prove it. Thor wasn't working on the wheels right now, though. He was under the hood, his convict-orange jumpsuit and blond hair bright against the shadows cast by the overhead lights. I put my chin on my knees, watching silently from the shadows. It wasn't as good as being up to my elbows in grease myself, but the smell of oil and gasoline was as soothing to me as mother's milk.

Not that anything about my mother was soothing. I stifled a groan and put my forehead against my knees, listening to the muffled cursing and good-natured banter that went on over the rumbles and squeaks of fixing cars. Tension ebbed out of my shoulders as the comfort sounds and smells vied with my mother's memory for priority in my thought process.

Sheila won out. The image of her pregnant kept invading the backs of my eyelids. She was prettier than I was, and looked serenely confident as she stared back at me from behind my eyes. I could all but see the wind picking up her hair, long black strands that whisked back from her face with a life of their own, but no matter how hard I tried to meet her eyes, I couldn't read any emotion in them. "Come on." I didn't think I was speaking aloud. I was talking to a memory of someone I'd never known. "Tell me what's going on, can't you? What's this guy want? You stopped him once, O Mystical Mother. Give me something to work with here."

She didn't. Evidently not even the memory of her responded well to sarcasm. I sighed and dropped my head farther against my knees. In the garage, metal bit into metal with a high-pitched squeal, a shriek that should have lifted hairs on my arms and made me shiver with discomfort. It had exactly the opposite effect, draining away tension from my neck and making my grip on my own arms slip a little, so that I slumped even more on the stairs. I'd spent far too much time in shops, listening to that sound, to find it uncomfortable. At least, not when I heard it someplace like the garage, where it belonged.

"It's a strange way you have of belonging."

That sound made me flinch, my fingers tightening around my arms again. I could still hear the scream of metal, although as I lifted my head it seemed to blend with a wuthering wind, no less eerie a sound.

Sheila MacNamarra, my very own mother, stood a few feet away, wearing the cable-knit sweater and jeans she'd worn in the photograph taken almost twenty-seven years ago. A silver necklace glinted in the hollow of her throat, all but hidden by the sweater. Her hair was lifted on the wind, moving slowly, as if time was being stretched thin and we were slipping between moments of it.

"Sure, and that's what's happening, now, isn't it?" She took a step forward, the blustery grey sky behind her super-imposed over the shop's girders and lights. "Siobhán Grania MacNamarra." My name sounded liquid and lovely in her accent, if I overlooked the fact that none of it was the name I considered mine. "You grew up so tall, my girl." Sheila curved her hand over her tummy and smiled at me. "Your father was tall."

"He still is." My voice was hoarse. I could see blowing grass around her knees, and a white two-story house in the middle of a field. I could also see, with a little more effort, the shop behind her. This was not like any of my limited experiences with worlds that were Other. As much as I wasn't crazy about those, at least I kind of knew what to expect from them. This was a whole new ball game. "Are you real?"

"That I am." Sheila crouched so that she was looking up at me on my stair. "So it's come 'round again, has it? We're back to where we began, you and I. How've we been, girl? Have we had a good life together?"

Cold shocked against my skin from the inside, making my cheeks burn. "What are you talking about? We haven't had any life together at all. You're dead."

Sheila's shoulders pulled back, her face blanching. "Am I now." She stood, hands pressed against her thighs, and took a few steps away. Her shoulder ended up lodged in the stairwell corner, which bothered the hell out of me and didn't seem to phase her at all. "And how long have I been dead?"

"About three months. What, you don't kn—" Wire contracted around my lungs, forcing air out as surely as a sword could. I rubbed the heel of my hand against my breastbone and tried to pull in a breath deep enough to snap the feeling of suffocation. "You don't know." My words had no strength behind them. "I'm talking to the you from thirty years ago."

"I told you, now, didn't I? That we were between moments of time." Sheila turned back to me, sudden urgency crackling in her movements. "And here I thought this was something done on purpose, but it's not, lass, is it? You've fallen through time and don't even know how you've done it. Have I been such a poor mother to you, then? Taught you nothing of the old ways? Ah, Siobhán, what's gone on?"

"My name is Joanne." Even as I spoke I saw the words cut her, something I hadn't intended. Her eyes lost some of their light and she fell back a step, lowering her gaze.

"I see. Joanne, then. It's a fine name, and isn't it though. Now tell me, girl. You called me, but I think it's my own skill that's brought me here, not yours." She frowned at me, faint and censuring. "I can see the power in you, but it's raw and untempered. I don't understand. You're a woman grown. You should be at the height of your skill by now."

"There's not really time to go into it right now, Mother. You stopped someone, a killer, right?" It was all coming out much more sharply than I meant it to, but I had no idea how to deal with this woman. There was softness in her, kindness. Love. It didn't fit with the mother I'd known, and I was afraid distraction would keep me from ever understanding what was going on. She was already dead. It seemed a little late for her to be getting the answers she needed. "He's back, or somebody like him is back. What's going on?"

I watched it happen. The gentleness drained from her, leaving behind something much colder and more stark. Lines that I hadn't seen in her face a second earlier now etched themselves around her mouth and between her eyebrows. The serenity washed away, leaving behind nothing more than resolution.

A wave of sickness and sorrow hit me in the stomach and overtook my whole body, making tears sting at the back of my eyes. My throat tightened up and my hands cramped from cold. The girl in the photograph was gone, and the woman I'd known as my mother had replaced her. I wanted to say I was sorry, to take the words back, because I'd liked the confused, light-voiced young woman from the photo, and I'd made her leave.

I was never going to escape that. With a handful of sentences, I'd taken the joy out of my own mother's heart and turned her into someone whose focus was so strong that she could will herself to death while I sat by her side and watched. The shriek of metal penetrated my awareness again, combining with the wind to scream in banshee cries that I thought would wake me up every night for the rest of my life.

"I've yet to fight the Blade. Those poor women, their lives lost and to no avail." Sheila curved both her hands over her belly now, then made fists of her hands. "Damn him, damn them both to Hell."

"Me?" There was something about an Irishman cursing someone to hell that carried far more conviction than an American making the same damnation. My voice came out a childish squeak, betraying a fear I thought should be absurd, but which seemed very real at that moment. Sheila jerked her head up, then yanked her hands away from her pregnant tummy.

"No." The softness was gone from the Irish lilt, leaving cold edges. "Not you, Siobhán. Joanne. I thought I had the strength to banish him and lock away his master forever, but there are things I will not risk."

"Me," I squeaked again. Sheila flattened her hand against the curve of her belly again, the gesture more than answer enough. My head began to pound, a throb that fit into the beats between the rise and fall of the wind and tearing metal. "You didn't stop this guy who rips out people's entrails for fun and profit because you were protecting me?"

"Sure and I thought I'd be stopping him, girl." Hard, dissonant notes sounded in my mother's voice. "I'd thought this plan through for so long. Break his power circle and push him so far out of time he'll be lost for good. But I can't follow him to the ends of the earth to make certain, for the life within me can't withstand the journey, my fragile Siobhán."

Time blurred with a squeal of sound, a too-fast babbling of voices being sped up. The light changed, winter sun dropping and darkening into night. Clouds whisking above Sheila faded to an ominous red, as if the shadow of an eclipse was slipping over them. Even the prosaic flourescent lights burning behind the memory of clouds began bleeding. I twisted in my stair seat, looking behind me at a low red moon. Dread prickled up through the soles of my feet, itching like bee stings, and spread higher into my body. The bleat of time fast-forwarding slowed, and avaricious malevolence crawled over me, pinning me in place like an unfortunate butterfly. My lungs filled with blood, pain slicing my cheek as I clapped my hand against a healed-over scar there. My fingers came away coated in red wetness.

A piece of darkness fell away from the crimson moon, plunging tip over tail to the earth. In the instant before it smashed to the ground, blackness flared and it became a man, or at least a thing that looked like a man. Emaciated and pale, it moved too smoothly to be human, gliding across the Irish field and through the garage walls faster than a man could run. My belly contracted, the knot of power hidden there flaring, ready to be used if I could think of a way to use it.

I couldn't think at *all*. The thing, the man—I saw in a flash of moonlight how sharp and narrow his features were, like the rest of him, and remembered that Sheila had called him the Blade. It seemed like a good name, and the choking sensation of blood in my lungs only brought home the accuracy of it. The Blade swept toward me, moving ever faster while I sat frozen, feeling as if I was wrapped in safety, unable to free myself even with the best of intentions. The Blade reached out long bony fingers, curling them as if he'd throttle me, and I sat and watched him do it.

Sheila MacNamarra did not. I never saw her move, but then, I was transfixed by the Blade and looking the other way. She put herself between me and him, a human woman vibrant with life. She flared golden, like a moment of starborn glory, and the Blade shrieked a sound of torn metal and moaning winds. He leaped forward, fingers clawed for her throat. She caught him with a foot in the stomach and they rolled ass over teakettle, thumping through the field and the bodies of police sedans.

I felt each jolt as they hit the ground, smashing through my body as if I was encased in water. Despite myself, I let go a little giggle: I felt no personal danger, only fascination and curiosity as I bounced around with the two combatants. I could feel Sheila gather her will and insist upon *change*. The air itself responded as she flung up her arm to block the Blade's attack. His hands crashed against a shield of air as solid as steel. Sheila scrambled to her feet, still wielding her invisible shield, and smashed it in a backhand swing, catching the Blade by the face and knocking him backward.

Again I felt her gather her will. Bars that I couldn't see but could sense began to spring up around the Blade. This wasn't just the essence of healing, the thing I'd been told I could do as a shaman. It was something more, something far beyond not just my capabilities, but even my skill to imagine. I watched, round eyed with admiration and astonishment, as the world seemed to leap at her command. *My mom can beat up your bad guy!* a little part of my mind crowed. I clamped a hand over my mouth to prevent another giggle from escaping.

The blood-red of the sky deepened like a warning bell. The Blade shot taller, more narrow, as if gaining strength from the wrongly colored world. Sheila faltered, a creature of light weakened by its absence. The Blade shrieked pleasure and crashed through the bars she'd built, shattering her will as if it was nothing. For the first time I saw her cower, a moment of weakness in the woman with an indomitable spirit.

I had nothing to give, but I had nothing to lose, either. I reached out to the place I sat in the real world, my garage, a place of safety and comfort to me, and begged for power to help save the woman who protected me. The very cars themselves seemed to respond, filling me with the knowledge that I was—or had been—one of their caretakers. The walls of the place, in a building meant to house those who safeguarded the city, gave to me what I asked, their own strength and certainty in the role they filled. For a moment it overwhelmed me, raw power from things that had seemed lifeless to me before.

Then the Blade was bearing down on Sheila, fingers locked around her throat, making her the fourth victim of his murdering spree. I took what I'd been granted and coiled it up with my own core of silver-blue power, then wound up and threw it overhand, like a baseball, into Sheila MacNamarra's hands.

Power erupted like an electric line cut loose, snapping and flailing. The Blade shot backward, landing dozens of yards away on hands and feet, still skidding back. Rocks in the field tore up under his long fingers, furrows grooved in the concrete garage floor. For an instant, the banshee cries stopped, leaving a silence so profound it hurt me in my bones.

Then even I saw the flash of silver thread that lay

between myself and the roundness of my mother's belly. It pulsed with the power I'd just thrown, crackling and popping like a trapped snake. The Blade's gaze snapped to me, focusing on me for the first time since Sheila had placed herself between us. He howled a victorious shriek and pounced toward me, forgetting Sheila in the moment of triumph. As he reached me, Sheila rose up behind him with her hands wrapped around a column of light, a weapon shaped from her own will and nothing more. She drove it into his spine, sending him arching backward with a scream that brought rupturing agony to my ears, and then blessed silence.

The blood red light cleared. I slithered down the last few steps into the garage, stickiness trickling from my ears. Sheila's face appeared above me, round eyebrows drawn down with concern, long black hair tucked behind her ears. She had her hand pressed over her stomach, fear narrowing her green eyes. Rushing clouds whirled behind her head, and I managed a tiny smile.

Relief swept her face, her lips shaping words I couldn't hear. I said, "Thank you," feeling the words vibrate in my throat even if they didn't echo in my ears.

Then her face blurred into Thor the Thunder God's, and I decided that was as good a time as any to pass out.

CHAPTER 6

I woke up to a weirdly silent world in which Morrison's face was hovering worriedly over mine. Morrison worried was distressing. Much more distressing than Morrison yelling. There were certain constants in my world.

Hearing, for example. Up until this very moment, hearing had been one of those constants. Now there was nothing. No ringing in my ears, no ocean of blood thrumming, no background traffic noises or cops arguing over topics ranging from doughnuts to politics.

One missing constant I could deal with. Two was too much. I frowned at Morrison and said, "Why aren't you yelling?"

At least, I think I did. I never realized how much I depended on hearing myself to know I was talking. I mean, I could feel my voice box working, but the astounding silence into which the words fell really, really made me want to begin shouting. I didn't, but only just barely. I thought shouting would look a lot like giving in to panic, and since it appeared that half the precinct was standing behind Morrison, I didn't want to come across like a wussy girl just because of a little thing like shattered eardrums.

I felt very much like a wussy girl just then. It was possible I owed Billy a very small apology for being bent out of shape over the one-of-the-guys comments. A very small apology. Minuscule. I closed my eyes, cleared my throat—another thing that I could only feel, not hear—and said, "I'm okay."

I got my eyes open again in time to see everybody sag with relief. Even Morrison, although he covered it nicely by scowling magnificently and, judging from the color of his face and the fact that I could see his uvula, yelling.

It made me feel a lot better about not being able to hear, actually. I sat up very slowly, not at all sure that broken eardrums didn't equate to a broken sense of balance. It didn't seem to, which was nice. Vomiting on my boss after all this fuss would have been embarrassing. Especially since he was being nice, and had a hand between my shoulder blades, keeping me steady as I sat.

"I'm okay," I repeated silently. "I just, ah..." Something tickled along my jaw. I reached up to scratch it and came away with sticky, drying blood under my fingernails. "I can't hear," I said to nobody in particular, especially myself, since I couldn't hear me, "and the thing we're after looks and sounds a lot like Munch's *Scream*."

I suspected I was glad I was looking at the gook under my nails instead of the gathered crowd. "I'm going to need a little time," I said, still to my icky fingers. "And maybe a sandwich."

The room cleared like I'd fired a shot. Ten seconds later the only people left were Morrison, Thor, and Billy, the middle of whom looked like he'd rather be somewhere else. "I'm fine," I told him. "Thanks for, um. Whatever you did."

He gave me a tight smile, nodded, and followed the rest of the crowd like he'd been given a reprieve from the firing squad. I wondered why my mind was wandering down the aisle of shooting similes. I'd never been completely deafened by firing a gun.

Billy looked at Morrison in a way that made me look, too. The captain said something I didn't catch—obviously—and Billy cast me a worried glance, then nodded and left the room. I finally figured out I was in the broom closet, which was nice. It was the station's flop room, kept meticulously clean for cops who'd been on the job too long and needed a rest break. I hadn't known it was big enough to hold more than two people, much less the eight or so that'd been in there.

Morrison touched my shoulder. I nearly jumped out of my skin, then drew in a sharp breath through my nose and turned to face him, eyes wide. Not hearing sucked a lot. He said something and I focused on his mouth, concentrating.

"If you think," he said, slowly and clearly enough for me to read, "that you're getting out of work today just because you collapsed with blood running from your ears, think again."

I had never heard—or not heard—such reassuring words in my life. I split a grin that turned into laughter, and leaned forward to give the police captain a hug. A tiny dimple that I'd never noticed before quirked at the corner of Morrison's mouth, and he returned the hug somewhat gingerly. I sat back, still grinning, and felt my face fall long and googly with dismay. "Oh, shit."

Morrison's eyebrows shot up and he followed my focus to his shoulder, where his formerly impeccably white shirt was now stained with sticky red residue. "Oh, for Christ's sake, Walker," he said, and he didn't even have to say it slowly for me to understand. I wrinkled up my face in apology. He sighed explosively and waved it off. "What the hell happened to you?"

"I ran into the bad guy." I was trying so hard not to shout that I suspected I was barely more than whispering.

"In the *garage*?"

It was amazing how easily I understood him. Amazing, and somewhat alarming. I frowned at his mouth and nodded, then shook my head. Not being able to hear made me feel like I wasn't able to talk, either.

"In Ireland. In the garage. It's complicated. Morrison, I'd really like to get my ears fixed before anything else happens."

"You think something else is going to happen?"

"Something else always happens."

His eyebrows rose and fell in an acknowledging shrug. "Do you need a doctor?"

I shook my head. "Just some time and some food." I felt like somebody'd turned me upside down and shaken every last bit of energy out of me. Thinking about it made it worse. Morrison's hand found its place at my spine again, supporting me, and it took everything I had to not lean over, curl my fingers in his shirt, and snivel on him for a minute. "I'm a little tired." That time my voice felt so low I wasn't at all sure I'd spoken out loud. Morrison tipped my chin up so I could see what he was saying. It struck me as an unbelievably intimate gesture, and I felt myself blushing. Morrison ignored it, which was somewhere between relieving and insulting.

"Lie back down, Walker. You're white as a sheet."

I *felt* white as a sheet. I felt like all the energy that I usually ignored had been bleached and left out to dry. Part of me wanted to argue, because Morrison was the one telling me what to do. The other part thought falling asleep for the rest of the day sounded like a good idea. I started to nod, but Morrison's finger under my chin kept my head from dropping.

"I sent Holliday to get your drum. That'll help, right?"

I nearly kissed him. Instead I closed my eyes and bit my lower lip, nodding. "Yeah. Thank you." My nose prickled with embarrassing tears. "Thanks."

I didn't hear him answer, but I felt the rumble of his voice through his touch.

"I'll just lie down until Billy gets here, or food does." I didn't need to hear my own voice, either, to know that it was full of stings and thorns; that was how my throat felt. I hoped I just sounded tired, not angry or about to burst into tears. Morrison wrapped a strong hand around my biceps and helped me lie back down. I pulled a pillow over my head and knew nothing for a little while.

BILLY DIDN'T JUST COME BACK with my drum. He came back with Gary, who found me in the laundry room, washing the broom-closet sheets. By the time he found me I'd eaten and rinsed out my ears, which made me feel considerably more human. I was leaning against the washing machine, feeling it do its thing, when Gary poked his head in and said something I couldn't hear. I grinned a little and pointed at my ear, which made him huff and puff like the big bad wolf.

Getting anything useful out of the drum when I couldn't hear proved to be awkward as hell. I eventually sat down directly across from Gary and kept my fingertips on the drum's edge while he knocked out a beat.

I'd never felt the drum actually call up energy inside me before. It was like a well filling, a few bubbles in the depth of me turning into splashes and then into a steady trickle. I said, "Faster," and Gary increased the beat until the power of the drum made me laugh with the feeling of life well lived. It was an entirely internal celebration that took my breath and made my blood run thinner and faster in my veins. I wanted a hundred drums all around me, so their vibrations shook the very air, making it safe for me to dance even without being able to hear the beat.

I burst through the top of my head and into clear sky so cold even the blue was leached from it. I could hear my own labored breathing as I tried to catch oxygen from the thin air, but I knew with great certainty that I was hearing an illusion. My spirit might be unharmed—at least with regards to this particular instance—but the body I'd left behind needed repair work.

The first analogy that slid through my mind was that of blown-out stereo speakers. I folded my legs and sat in the clear thin air, just as I might have within my own garden, and began the process of removing the destroyed stereo components and replacing them. I overlaid the idea on my own body, and called for the renewed power that lay coiled inside me. It sprang up, eager for the call, and swept through me.

I had a completely horrid sensation in both my ears at once, as if bugs were crawling out of them. I stuck a finger in one and wriggled it, coming away with a tiny smear of bloody flesh. I let out a ragged yell and flapped my hand frantically, getting rid of the icky bit, then repeated the whole ritual, including the frantic flapping, on the other side.

That part didn't hurt.

The next part did. I could feel the power in me rebuilding my eardrums, fitting the right amount of newly created flesh into the cavity in my ear. It felt like an ink-jet printer was zipping back and forth inside my ear, making one tiny line of new eardrum after another. Heat ran down my eustachian tubes and into the back of my throat, tasting like blood and feeling increasingly like someone had poured molten gold into the delicate tubes.

I kept coughing and trying to gag the feeling away. Nothing worked, the boiling feeling continuing to zip around in my ears, until they popped abruptly and wind shrieked against my new eardrums. I fell back inside my head, the ringing of the drum suddenly impossibly loud, and yelled again, this time scaring the bejeezus out of Gary, who stopped drumming and threatened me with the drumstick. Then he leaned over the drum and hugged me without warning, mumbling, "You get in all kinds of trouble when I'm not around, lady. You oughta watch yourself."

"Yeah, well, you should see the other guy." I wrinkled my face. "Actually, I guess that's the problem. We can see him now."

"Am I s'posed to understand that?"

I gave him a lopsided smile. "Not really. C'mon. I need to go talk to Billy."

"MY MOTHER CALLED it the blade. Blade." I tried it out without a capital letter and with one, wrinkling my nose. "Its master's blade, specifically."

"And its master is?"

I shrugged. Billy looked at the ceiling like he was asking strength from God. I spread my hands. "I thought getting any kind of name from a woman who's been dead for three months was pretty good."

"Well, can you go get more?"

I slid down in my chair, glaring futilely at Billy's computer screen. "What have I done for you lately, huh?"

"It's the nature of the beast, Joanie. Can't get no satisfaction." He gave me a sideways look. "Are you really okay?"

"Right as rain." I scratched my jaw where the blood had been. "I don't know how real this thing is, Bill. I'm not sure if it's something you can catch. Whatever Mother did to it set it back a lot of years, but she thought she'd have the power to destroy it, and that was a big fat bust. And whatever it is has got a master."

"Forget about the master. The master isn't the thing stringing girls out by their guts, right?"

"Right." God, I hoped I was right.

"Then he's not our problem right now. By the way, Melinda wants to know if you're still coming over for dinner."

I blinked. "What?"

"It's the equinox tonight. She invited you last week, remember?"

"And you think to bring this up in the context of masters? Or was it being strung out by your guts?"

Billy fashioned a crooked grin. "You know Mel. She's a slave driver."

I laughed. "So a little bit of both. Yeah, I don't see why not. I mean, you tell me. I know it's the first forty-eight hours of a murder investigation that are most critical, but we're kind of way the hell past that. Is taking the night off going to make a critical difference?"

"If it does, it's my ass in the hot seat, not yours. You're just a beat cop, remember?"

"A beat cop who isn't doing her job today. Crap." I got to my feet. "Did Morrison put somebody on the Ave to cover for me, or am I going to get beaten within an inch of my life the next time he sees me?"

"You're fine, Joanie." Billy's voice was gentle. "People who spontaneously rupture eardrums, even if they follow it up with a little lay-your-hands-on-me action, are generally considered out for the day."

I sat back down. "Yeah? That happens enough to have a protocol for it?" Probably only with me around. Great. "Can I bring Gary to dinner? Petite's still in the shop."

Billy looked around. "Where'd he go?"

"Back to work. Some of us," I said in my best gruff Gary voice, "gotta work for a living, darlin'."

"Oh. Sure, bring him. Mel cooks enough to feed an army anyway."

"That's because you have four kids, Billy. That *is* an army." I scooted forward, nodding at his computer. "Okay, so I'm Detective Holliday's personal assistant for the day, I guess. What do you want me looking for?"

Billy snorted. "I can look up weird shit on the Net, Joanie. You're the one with the direct line to higher powers."

"Jesus H. Christ on a pogo stick, Billy. Don't say things like that. Higher powers my ass." I actually shuddered.

"Whatever you want to call it, you've got a bead on something I can't access. Even the captain knows it."

A fact which did not fill me with joy and glee. I sighed, dropping my chin to my chest. "Last time I went into the wonderful world of the weird, my eardrums exploded, Billy."

"Look at it this way. At least nobody shoved a sword through your lung." He gave me a sunny smile that held up to the glare I shot his way.

"Thank you. Thank you, Billy, that really helped a lot. Bastard."

"Hey." Billy looked injured. "My parents were married."

"Mine weren't." Huh. I'd never thought of myself as a bastard before. Interesting, what you can get through almost twenty-seven years of living without thinking. "Look, Billy?" I heard myself get all quiet, like I was about to impart something important. Billy heard it, too, and leaned forward.

"My mother had the chance to eliminate this guy back when she faced him. She didn't because she was pregnant with me and she didn't want to risk me. So this whole thing is kind of my fault." I wrapped my arms around my ribs, staring at a broken corner of tile beneath Billy's desk. "I mean, the fact that there are more dead women now. I know I'm being sort of a jerk, because I hate all this crap, but...I really want to get this thing solved. I need to. Whatever it takes."

Billy clapped his hand on my shoulder, solid and reassuring. "We'll figure it out, Joanie. We'll get this guy. You'll get your piece."

Or maybe he said *peace.* I wasn't sure.

CHAPTER 7

The drumming hadn't been enough to fill me up. Not all the way, at least. Maybe a hundred drums would've poured so much energy and power into me that I'd have been good to go for the rest of the day, the rest of the week, as long as it took. But by mid-afternoon I was stumbling like Petite did when she ran short on gas, and nothing I did brought me even one whit closer to figuring out what the Blade was or how to stop him from killing someone else.

So I did what any sensible woman would do. I went—no, not shopping. My idea of an ideal shopping experience was walking into the store, finding exactly what I wanted on the first rack I stopped at, buying it, and being out of there in five minutes. I was a retailer's nightmare.

But I was also a well-trained Seattleite. When the chips were down, I went for coffee.

The Missing O was half a block down the street from the precinct building, run by an entrepreneurial young fellow who thought the idea of opening a doughnut and coffee shop next to a police station was pretty funny. After a while the cops started thinking it was funny, too, and began to take a certain pride in being the O's number-one clientele.

A barista greeted me not by name, but by drink: "Tall hot chocolate with a shot of mint?" I waved an agreement and went to pay without ever having to say anything. A minute later I was ensconced in the corner, hands wrapped around the drink.

A coffee shop with a mug of hot chocolate was no place to solve the world's problems from, but it beat a sharp stick in the eye. I let my eyes half close, watching the world through a blur of lashes and waiting for inspiration to strike.

Inspiration, last I checked, did not come in the form of Captain Michael Morrison. Well. He was certainly inspiring in some ways. He frequently inspired me to mouth-frothing argument, for example. At the moment, though, he stood a few feet away, frowning down at me as if unsure how to approach. I untangled my eyelashes and looked up at him. "I don't bite." I thought about that statement, then nodded, determining it was true. I couldn't remember having bitten anyone in my sentient years.

Morrison let out a fwoosh of air and shrugged his shoulders. He was wearing a seaman's coat with big black buttons, so out of fashion it looked like haute couture. "That's a great coat."

He looked as startled as I felt. To the best of my recollection, nothing like a compliment had ever passed my lips when I was speaking to the captain. He shrugged again, hands in his pockets, which made the whole coat move like a woollen wall with a purpose in life, and sat down. "Thanks. Belonged to my father."

"Seriously?" I supposed it was unlikely Morrison had

sprung fully formed from the forehead of his mother, but I'd never given much thought to his family. "He was a sailor?"

"Merchant marines. He died when I was twelve."

Neither of us knew what to say after that. I slid down in my seat and wrapped my fingers around my hot chocolate tightly enough to bend the cardboard. "So," I said after a while, just as he said, "Your hearing's back." I twitched a grin at the plastic top of my cup and nodded. I didn't see if Morrison smiled, too.

"You and Holliday learn anything yet?"

"We would've mentioned it if we had." It came out sarcastic. I hadn't meant it to. I saw Morrison's bulk move back a few centimeters, like he was responding to my nasty tone and putting extra space between us. *Good, Joanne. Antagonize the boss. Again.* "I'm trying, Captain. I really am."

He muttered, "You certainly are," under his breath, making me look up in amused offense. His expression hadn't changed. Maybe I was the only one who thought he was making a joke. Great. Just great.

"I really want to solve this." I kept my voice low, afraid he'd think I was kidding. After a moment something relaxed in his gaze, a little gleam of approval coming into it. I annoyed Morrison for a variety of reasons, starting with knowing a lot more about cars than he did, and ending, emphatically, with wanting a career as a mechanic when it was his opinion I could be a good cop. It was possible I'd taken one tiny baby step toward a better relationship with him by genuinely wanting to solve this case.

"Has it occurred to you that you might be in danger, Walker?"

The chocolate was hot enough to keep my fingers stinging with warmth, or I'd have dropped it in my lap, hands suddenly numb from surprise. "Sir?" I never called Morrison *sir*. I don't know which of us liked it less.

"Your mother turned this killer in thirty years ago. If he puts you together with her—"

I sat there staring at him, slack jawed with stupefaction. "It's unlikely," I finally heard myself say. "Different country, different names, pretty much no connection...."

"Except whatever the hell you've got going on up there." Morrison pointed a thick finger at my head. I touched my own temple guiltily. The man had a point. Crap. He had a point, and I had no idea what to do if he was right. I blinked at the table, hoping it might come up with a brilliant answer or two.

"Is this going to turn out like the last case?"

Then again, maybe I hadn't taken any steps toward him approving of me at all. I curled a lip at the top of my hot chocolate, doing my best James Dean impression. "You mean with a dead body and no actual proof of guilt aside from the word of a semi-hysterical teenage girl?"

Morrison gave a credible growl that rumbled up from the depths of his chest. I took that as a yes, and shrugged uncomfortably. "I'm putting my money on 'probably.'"

Silence stretched over the table long enough to break. I looked up when it snapped, to find Morrison glaring out the window, his mouth set in a thin line. At least he wasn't glaring at me. "Get me some answers, Walker. Tell me how to stop somebody else from dying."

I lowered my gaze to the cup again. "For what it's worth, Morrison, I don't like this any more than you do."

He stood up, the chair feet squeaking back against the wet floor. "That's the only thing that makes it bearable."

I didn't feel any less alone, watching him leave, shoulders broad and strong in the seaman's coat.

. . .

I LOCKED myself in the broom closet back at the station and struggled to get inside my own mind. When I finally did, my garden looked like somebody had dumped ash all over it, making it as tired and grey as I felt. It was not reassuring. Nor was the fact that it took Coyote a very long time indeed to show up, or that he looked distracted when he did. How a dog could look distracted, I didn't know, but there you had it.

"I'm not," he said for the umpteenth time, "a dog."

One of the few thoughts I seemed to be able to keep to myself around him was the private glee at being able to get on his nerves with something as simple as calling him a dog. It made me feel better right away. I even managed a bright grin. "Sorry. I need your help."

"God helps those who help themselves, Joanne."

I startled. "What, you're a Christian now?"

"Is that so strange?"

"Is it strange that my shape-shifting coyote spirit guide is a Christian? You tell me."

He finally looked at me, little spots of brighter-colored fur above his eyes lifting like eyebrows. "No," he said. "It's not. You've got too many preconceptions, Walkingstick."

"I wish you people would stop calling me that." I didn't like having my original last name bandied around. Especially not when I was dealing with psychic realms I didn't really understand. The idea that names had power was one I could grasp, if nothing else. Which actually brought me to my point: "I need to know how to protect myself, Coyote."

He snapped his teeth at me and got up to pace toward me, looking alarmingly like a predator instead of a scavenger. "You should've been learning that for most of the last three months."

"So sue me. Are you going to throw me to the wolves just because I'm slow on the uptake?" More than slow, I admitted. One might go so far as to say recalcitrant. Deliberately recalcitrant.

I could live with that.

At least, I could live with it as long as he gave me the help I needed now. Possibly, very possibly, this was not a good long-term game plan. I promised myself I'd think about that later. Preferably much later. I did my best puppy-dog eyes on Coyote.

Note to self: puppy-dog eyes work better on people who do not actually possess puppy-dog eyes themselves. Coyote looked disgusted. I retreated on the puppy-dog defense and tried a verbal one. "All I need to know is how to protect the very core part of me, Coyote. My name. That kind of thing. I don't want the bad guys to be able to get to it easily."

"A thought which only strikes you now that a bad guy is looming."

"Yeah."

Coyote dropped his head in a very human motion, and sighed so deeply I was surprised he didn't start coughing. "You know how to do it, Joanne. Think in metaphors."

"What?" I found myself grinning just a little. "Like airbags and steel frames keeping my little ol' name safe?"

He gave me a look that would reduce a lesser woman to blushes of embarrassment. I valiantly ignored the burning in my cheeks and mumbled, "Oh."

"I don't know why I put up with you." He snapped his teeth at me again, and was gone.

"Because I'm cute and irresistibly charming," I said to

the empty garden. No one, not even a mockingbird, responded.

"Please tell me dinner isn't going to suck as much as the rest of today has." I leaned over the top of Billy's computer, sighing. He looked up, offended.

"Are you dissing Mel's cooking?"

I snorted a laugh. "No. I just feel useless." I put my hands on his desk, letting my head hang. "Find anything about the Blade?"

Billy let out an explosive sigh and creaked back in his chair, hands folded behind his head. "Comic book references. Stuff about some swordsman named Bob Anderson. Wesley Snipes pictures."

"Really?" I perked up, edging around his desk to try to get a look at the screen. "Any half-naked ones?"

"Joanie!"

I drooped. "I didn't think so. There wasn't nearly enough half-naked Wesley in those movies, anyway."

Billy gave me a flat look. "Any luck with the psychic stuff?"

My cheeks went hot with discomfort. "No. I...can't get there." My jaunt to see Coyote had tapped me out. I couldn't get any further out of my body than your average caterpillar could. In fact, a caterpillar, with its whole transformation process, was probably going to have more success than I was right now.

"Oh." Billy's silence stretched out a few long moments. "All three of the dead women are from the greater Seattle area," he said eventually. "The Captain went to visit their families. To tell them. I was hoping we'd have something for him when he got back."

"Way to lay the guilt on, Billy." I slumped again, my head heavy enough to strain my neck. "All right. Look. I'm going to go down to the park and, um..." I wet my lips. "You remember that thing I did in the garage in January?"

Billy let out a huff of laughter. "How could I forget?"

"A lot of people seem to have. Or they're trying hard to." I shook my head. "I thought maybe I'd try something like that again down at the park. Having you along would be helpful. You, uh. Know how to put your energy out there." Pulling my tongue out with forceps would have been more fun than saying that sentence. Billy, bless his pointy little head, didn't laugh. He just stood up and grabbed his coat.

FRESH SNOW GLITTERED over paths that had been stomped down by a lot of police officers in the past twenty-four hours. The sky was clearing, leaden grey clouds parting to let sparks of sunlight through. I squinted at the ground, kicking up sprays of snow as I tromped through the park, a few steps ahead of Billy.

I could feel Billy walking behind me on a more than physical level. In January I'd asked people to offer up their energy to help me net a god. Billy was getting ready to do that again, coiling his own essence into a ball that he'd be able to share with me when I needed it. Not, I thought, unlike what I'd done for my mother, in the memory/dream connection that morning. I blurted, "Sheila didn't defeat that thing by herself," filling up the silence of the snow-covered field with my voice. "I was there."

"Of course you were there." Billy sounded confused. "She was pregnant with you."

"No, I mean, I was there...twice." Such a gift I had for

explanation. "He was kicking her ass. I threw her some power. It went right through...me...into her."

"You boosted your fetal self so your mom could draw enough power to defeat the Blade?"

Billy made it sound so succinct and sensible that I had to look over my shoulder at him to see if he was kidding. He wasn't. I nodded. "Yeah. And then he noticed me, the adult me, and came after me, which distracted him enough that Sheila could...get him." I didn't really know what she'd done, besides stab a sword of light through his spinal cord. Maybe that was enough to set your average evil minion back thirty years.

"So," Billy said, "when you've got this time-travel thing down pat, you want to slip back to about, oh, '85 and tell me to invest in Microsoft?"

I laughed. "Only if you promise to share the proceeds with me." I hunched my shoulders, trying to rid myself of the itchy sensation between the shoulder blades. My interference with Sheila's confrontation twenty-seven years ago felt important. I just wasn't sure why.

I bounced off a wall that wasn't there and crashed back into Billy's chest. He oofed, catching me, then frowned down at me. "Joanie?"

"I have no fucking clue." I put my hand out and encountered resistance. I prodded, then stepped forward and leaned into it, feeling like a mime. Billy fought a grin and completely lost the battle.

"Gonna grow up to be Marcel Marceau?"

"I sure as hell hope not. Can you, um...?"

Billy, showing a remarkable ability to understand Jo-speak, edged around me and walked through the wall I'd hit. He turned, eyebrows lifted.

"Shit," I said in my best thoughtful tone. And, "What

the fuck." Apparently crashing into invisible walls brought out the naughty words in me. Curious, I pulled my glove off and put my hand against it directly.

A dangerous burst of dull red flashed around the entire baseball diamond, so quickly it was gone almost before I registered it. A tingle of malicious familiarity made the nerve in my elbow ache.

Morrison was right. The Blade had found a way to recognize me.

CHAPTER 8

"Joanie?" Billy stepped back through the barrier as if it wasn't there. I leaned harder on it, prodding at it with my hands and trying to do the same with my mind. It failed miserably. I did not think of my mind as a poking instrument. There was no scalpel-like wit here, no sharp-as-a-knife insights. Nor could I come up with a car analogy that would let me slide through the wall. Cars and walls, in my experience, smashed together, not phased through one another. Not that I'd ever smashed up a car myself. Petite was the only vehicle I'd ever owned and I'd have killed myself before running her into anything.

"Joanie?" Billy asked again. I took my hand off the wall, my nerve quieting as soon as I broke the contact.

"I can't get through." Obviously. "He put up some kind of firewall."

"A firewall."

"Yeah, you know. To keep unfriendlies out of your computer network?"

"I know what a firewall is, Joanie. I'm just questioning your usage. How come it let me through, if it's a firewall?"

I lifted my eyebrows at him. "It doesn't recognize you as an unfriendly. It's programmed for me." It was a *lot* easier to think in terms of computer protocols than magic. I thought I might be on to something here.

"Right. So can you still do the thing you were going to do?"

I pursed my lips and looked through the invisible barrier. "One way to find out." The core of power in me was waking up, the wall providing some kind of challenge it felt ready to stand up to. I was pretty sure it was a false high, but I was willing to take it.

"Last time I did this," I said, more to myself than Billy, "it didn't actually do a damned bit of good."

"You're older, wiser, and stronger now." There was an unexpected resonance to Billy's voice, a depth of faith that I knew full well I didn't deserve. Still, it made me straighten my shoulders and drag in a deep breath of cold air. I closed my eyes momentarily, feeling the steam from my breath beading into water on my eyelashes.

When I opened them again, I wasn't quite in my own body anymore. The core of silver-blue energy was alive inside me, pushing me out as though there wasn't enough room for the two of us in this town. For a moment I felt like I was being given a gift I didn't really deserve: I hadn't done any of the training Coyote thought I should, and I wasn't sure I ought to be able to slip out of my body so easily.

The flip side to that, equally frightening, was that if I could do it without any training, then maybe he was right, and it really was something I should be doing with my life. I didn't like that possibility any better at all.

Right in front of me, the Blade's firewall glimmered dark red, like blood seeping out from the heart of the world. It cut off my ability to see anything inside it with more than ordinary eyes. I turned my head very slowly, unsure if my body was doing the same thing, but afraid to move too quickly for fear of jarring myself out of the double vision. Beyond the firewall, the world was full of neon colors, pulses of life that looked like a kid with fingerpaints had gone wild. Billy was just to my right, a swirling ball of orange and fuchsia energy held in his hands. I whispered, "Thanks," and though I was pretty sure I hadn't said it out loud, he crooked a grin and nodded his head once in acknowledgment. I reached out for his colors, calling them to me as politely as I could. They leaped out of his hands, whirling together like agitated kittens, and spun into the silver and blue core of me.

I felt, instantly, a dozen times stronger. My mind cleared, focus spilling through my limbs as if the blood had just remembered that it was supposed to be running. I didn't expect the sudden boost in clarity. It suggested my power really hadn't recovered from the run-in with the Blade that morning. Or almost thirty years ago. Whichever. The point was, if Billy's energy was bringing the world into that much sharper relief, I was even more tapped than I'd thought.

Buoyed by his dancing fuchsia and brilliant orange, I spread my hands, sending tentacles of power darting over the Blade's shield. Silver slithered over red, trailing my and Billy's colors like banners, testing and tracing the barrier. I went up, not around, looking for weak points that would allow me to hack into the system.

Giggling while out of body was an interesting experience. It felt like champagne bubbles in my nose and fingertips, little sparkles of glee that didn't require containment.

As if in response to my laughter, the red wall faltered.

My giggles cut off as I jumped to take advantage of the

weakness, a thin spot in the barrier that began to strengthen again even as I slid threads of power into it. I envisioned taloned nails that could grasp and tear more efficiently than my own, and worried at the spot like a determined rodent. I found myself grinning again, wondering what Coyote would think of me throwing over the car analogy in favor of using psychic rats to claw my way through a magical firewall. Even as I grinned, a silver tendril punched its way through the wall. Other colors, Billy's and mine both, leaped to the spot, squirming through and braiding together to strengthen each other without ever blending or losing any of their own distinctive coherence.

My hands lifted of their own accord, making claws that wrenched apart from one another, as though prying open a bear trap. The wall above me groaned and then tore, great jagged chunks ripping free with the same metal-on-metal shrieks I'd encountered that morning.

I was abruptly very cold, sweat standing out on my face and beading into my eyes. A dispassionate part of my mind suggested *shock?* and for a dizzying moment I considered stopping before I found myself face first in a snowbank, dying of exposure. The power I was using gasped and shriveled, the jaws I'd forced open in the red wall beginning to crash shut again. My knees gave out and I dropped to the snow. The chill helped me focus, and I used the energy that had been keeping me on my feet to try to keep the wall torn asunder. It had life of its own, forced and vicious, with no purpose beyond keeping me out. Destroying me, if it could.

And it was going to. I crumpled farther into the snow, pressure bearing down on my weakening breach in the wall like so much newspaper. I knotted my fingers in snow, feeling icy chunks bite into the lines of my ungloved hand

and then melt into bone-aching cold. I was going to be pulverized by someone who wasn't even there. What an embarrassing way to die.

At least Morrison wasn't there to see it. For a moment I went in a mental circle, annoyed that that was my last thought, then realizing it couldn't be, because *this* was my last thought—

Power slammed into me, drawn from a depth that I could barely fathom. Deep purple, burnt sienna—Billy's colors, but at their most profound. I could feel the love he drew on, lacing his colors with such gladness I was happy to stop breathing, so long as I could do it for *them*—

I didn't come to my feet. My body was irrelevant, left behind as I sprang forward on the force of the power Billy gave to me, unstinting. I slammed my fingers, all swirled with dominant purple, into the barely existent crack—all that was left of my opening in the wall—and tore it apart.

Redness shattered all around me, breaking in huge chunks of raw-edged power that collapsed into fragments as they hit the ground. I boiled through the opening and stood against the waves of blood rage that had gone into the killings. The bodies were gone, but the black power that linked one woman to another was still there, seeped in the earth beneath the snow like their blood. I could see lines that hadn't been there the day before—or that I hadn't been strong enough to see. Billy's outpouring of energy made my skin tingle, even if I'd left my actual body behind.

He can't keep this up forever, Joanne. Stop fucking around. Did other people have little voices in their heads that said things like that? I could stretch myself out a little and touch a hundred thousand minds in Seattle just to find out, but I was afraid the answer would be no. I refrained, instead focusing on the thin lines rising up from each of the three points where the women had died.

They came together in thready blackness, like oil-smeared string that glimmered and twisted with unhealthy light, making three points of a pyramid. They joined at the apex and braided together, reaching higher until the braid grew watery and distant. I could see it cut through the clouds and into the blueness of the sky beyond, but it faded before it reached the dark curve of space above the world. I was almost certain it faded, not that my vision was failing. The power diamond wasn't complete. The Blade needed one more body to finish building his stairway to heaven. That was the good news.

The bad news was it obviously didn't matter that the bodies themselves were gone. The power their deaths had bought was there, seared into the ground. Taking the three women away from the park hadn't broken the spell, and I wasn't sure what would.

The worst news was I could only think of one way to find out. The rich colors of Billy's power hadn't faded at all, memories coalescing around me: moments of love, laughing until the tears came; moments of holding sick children, afraid of what the night might bring. The bright spark of his wife's smile; the open acknowledgment that his girls had him wrapped around their little fingers, that his boys made him puff up with a fatherly pride he felt a little silly about, in this enlightened day and age.

What he was giving me was the part of him that would never, could never, give up. It was his center, his family, the core of all his strength, and just as surely, the center of all his weaknesses. He embraced every bit of it, flinging it toward me with everything he had, giving me the power to reach all the way to the stars. He knew what he was doing:

he could protect himself from the lethal drain but chose not to. Instead he offered up power far beyond the limits of safety. I could take it and follow the Blade's black thread into the heart of its darkness, and learn what lay behind him.

This morning and almost thirty years ago, my mother had had the same choice.

I fell back into my body with a jolt so hard it made my teeth ache, refusing the maelstrom of power offered to me by my friend. Refusing to take what he would give until the moment his system went into critical failure. I wouldn't take it, not even to fight the thing that wielded the murderous Blade.

Weak with exhaustion, I was still able to turn in time to catch Billy as he fell, the very life of him drained almost to the sticking point.

THE EARTH itself had power to spare, a thin green-and-blue flow far beneath its frozen surface. I reached for it with a worn-out plea, dragging the offered trickles of energy up through the snow and into myself. I couldn't reach even as far as the scattered trees, much less beyond the park's boundaries to beg for some of Seattle's teeming life energy. I had to wait, bent over Billy's chilled form, drawing in tiny spurts of strength until the swirling core of silver-blue inside me gave a little groan, and let power flow into my hands.

I fell back on the analogies I knew best. Billy's battery was drained and needed a jump. The thought of jumping Billy made me burble a snicker. His wife would beat me up.

The logical side of my mind said that if part of a person was the battery, it would probably be his mind. My hands drifted over Billy's heart without paying any attention to the logical part of my mind. I actually made little pinchers of my fingers, like jumper-cable heads, and clumsily stabbed one hand against my own heart, the other staying over Billy's.

It was a long and slow transfer of strength, my eyes half-shut and my head bowed over his. I was gaining very little for myself; what I could draw from the frozen ground beneath the snow I simply siphoned into Billy. His color improved gradually and he finally chuckled, more shaking his body than sounding in my ears. "Think we can walk out of here if we lean on each other?"

"Mngrnf." I thought that was supposed to be "maybe." Billy seemed to understand, and we took a couple of long minutes to climb to our feet, giggling with exhausted clumsiness.

"You find anything out?" he asked once we were both on our feet.

"Yeah." I tried out this whole walking thing, one shaky step. I could feel weary relief spill through him and into me.

"What?" His first step wasn't any steadier than mine. I smiled wearily and pulled myself up a little straighter, letting him lean on me.

"I found out I've got the best friends in the world. C'mon. Let's go, Holliday. Your wife's expecting us for dinner."

CHAPTER 9

"I swear on my wife's grave." Gary herded me up the stairs to Billy's front door, maneuvering Billy into line behind me. Mel stood in the open doorway, looking bemused. Gary spoke to her, not to me or Billy, which was just as well, because we'd gone well past punch-drunk sometime in the past hour of work and were howling with laughter every time anybody moved. "I swear on Annie's grave," Gary repeated to Mel, "this ain't my fault. They were like this when I picked 'em up at the station."

"I'd ask why Billy wasn't driving," Melinda said, getting out of her husband's way as he snickered and staggered through the door, "but I think I see why. I'm Melinda Holliday." She threaded a hand between me and Billy to shake Gary's, then fixed me with a gimlet eye. "Have you two been out drinking, Joanie?"

An eruption of giggles escaped through my nose and squirted tears from my eyes. I clapped both hands over my mouth and tried to wiggle a finger up to clear my eyes. "No. Swear to God. Hi, Mel." I bent to give her a hug, hoping I wouldn't lose my balance in doing so. She was nearly an entire foot shorter than I was and better dressed than anybody I'd ever met, including Billy. "This's my friend Gary. Gary Muldoon. He," I said extravagantly, "is a *hero*."

"Where 'hero' equates to 'designated driver'?" Melinda asked archly. "Get in here, all of you." She sounded like she was herding cats, or her four children. We all straightened up and scurried inside to the best of our ability, more obediently than either cats or her kids would have done.

"Joooooooaaaaanne!"

That was the last thing I heard before I went down in a pile of elbows and knees and squirming bodies. "Oh, sure," I heard Billy say, somewhere above my head. "Joanie gets all the hugs, but your old man gets nothing?"

"We see you all the time, Dad," a voice from the pile of squirmy people on top of me pointed out. The oldest kid—Robert-who-didn't-like-to-be-called-Bobby, that-was-a-little-boy's-name—extracted himself from the pile to give Billy a proper hug. He was eleven, not quite old enough to have too much dignity to show such blatant affection.

That left two kids squishing me, and one toddler slapping his barefoot way down the hall with the clear intention of finishing off the dog pile. Melinda scooped that one up, eliciting a howl of dismay while the girls, Jacquie and Clara, clambered off me, pulled me to my feet, and attached themselves to my sides like leeches. "Joanne, we haven't seen you since *forever*...how come you don't come over more often...did I show you my friendship pins...no I want to show her my Xbox it's cooler than the dumb pins—"

I didn't even know which of them wanted to show me what, but I promised, as loudly as I could, that I wanted to see both the pins and the Xbox and anything else they had to show me, which satisfied Clara, who released me and went tearing off down the hall shouting about the computer games. I grinned after her and gave Jacquie an extra hug. She beamed and clung to my side even more enthusiastically. I had no idea why they liked me so much, but I adored them and it made me feel I'd done something right in a prior life.

Except, the annoying little voice in my head said, brightly, *you haven't had any. That's what Coyote told you, remember?*

I told the annoying voice to shut up and tried to get my boots off without letting go of Jacquie. It was partly self-preservation; I still wasn't doing so well at the whole stand-ing-on-my-own thing, and neither, it seemed, was Billy, who leaned against the now-closed door and smiled wearily. This was what he needed more than any power I could have jumped his battery with: the rambunctious noise and love of his family.

Erik, the toddler, yowled, "Dooowwn!" and then added, in a snuffle, "Pease?" Melinda laughed and put him down. He crawled over to my feet through the snow we'd tracked in and helpfully began yanking on my shoelaces.

I'd been ushered out of the hall and into the kitchen, and had a glass of wine in my hand before I was entirely sure I'd gotten my boots off. Erik came trundling after us with one of the boots wrapped in his arms, which I took as more or less a good sign. Mel was exchanging pleasantries about it being nice to meet you with Gary, who scooped Jacquie—she was only five—off the floor and turned her upside down. Jacquie shrieked with unholy glee, narrowly missing kicking Gary in the nose. For an old guy with no kids of his own, he ducked well.

The first sip of wine hit me behind the eyes like a bowling ball. I let slip a startled giggle and lifted the glass to peer at it, as if I might see a miniature bottle of whiskey hidden in the rich dark liquid.

"Are you all right, Joanne?" Mel somehow heard my giggle through the general noise and turned to look at me, her eyebrows lifted and a teasing smile in place. "What have you and Bill been up to?"

"All kinds of weird sh—tuff." I caught myself just in time, but Robert, sitting on the counter where he wasn't supposed to be, smirked and rolled his eyes as if to say, *grown-ups.* Mel, without having to look his way, said, "Off the counter, Rob. Go set the table," which was apparently his punishment for thinking himself superior to adults. He thumped down with another eye-roll and I winked at him in sympathy as he skulked into the dining room. "We've been misbehaving horribly," I assured Mel. "I'll tell you about it after dinner."

"You'd better. I get huffy when strange women bring my husband home acting drunk on holidays."

"I'm not that strange," I protested. She laughed and went to open the kitchen window, sending a blast of cooler air into the hot room. I stepped closer to it, taking a deep breath as I leaned over the sink and peered at their backyard. It looked like a Thomas Kincaid painting, down to giant snowmen and half-buried swing sets. Moonlight turned it all purpley-blue. I lifted a toast to the man in the moon, the hard edges of his full disc reddened and mellowed by the wine in my glass.

"You're pretty strange, Jo," Gary said.

I looked back over my shoulder. "You're not helping."

He shrugged, grinning, and turned to Melinda. "Anything I can do to help, ma'am?"

"You could start by not calling me 'ma'am,'" Melinda suggested. I shook my head.

"Don't say that. He'll start calling you 'dame' and 'lady' and 'broad' if you're not careful."

"It's parta my charm," Gary said. I laughed.

"You keep saying that."

"And you keep hangin' around. I figure I must be right."

Melinda arched a curious eyebrow at me. I put my nose in my wineglass, suddenly aware that my cheeks were staining pink from something other than the warmth of the kitchen. I heard her under-the-breath, "Mmm-hmm," before she clapped her hands together, making herself the picture of efficiency. "All right. Joanne, you get the roast beef, Gary, you can get the potatoes. Jacquie, get in here, thank you dear, would you get the corn and where's your sister? Erik, not under the table, sweetheart. Erik, not under the—Erik! Get out from under the table!" She went to pull her errant child from beneath the dining room table while Gary and I followed Jacquie around, all of us picking up our charged items.

"I don't know how she does it," I whispered to Gary. "Four of them. I can't even find my own shoes some mornings."

"That's 'cause you leave 'em in the bathroom."

"Gary, how do you *know* that?"

He gave me an unrepentant grin and put the potatoes down on the table as he headed back into the kitchen. I put the roast beef down and smacked a hand against my forehead. Robert appeared at my elbow, looking curious. "Is he your boyfriend?"

"No!"

Robert got a grin that looked suspiciously like his mother's, said, "Uh-huh," and sauntered off. I had the distinct feeling I'd been had.

"You can sit next to *me*," Jacquie announced from

behind me. I spun around, blinking down at her. At least she probably wouldn't tease me about Gary.

"Okay. Where are we sitting?"

"Here and here." She dragged two chairs out and looked at me expectantly. I sat and she scrambled into her own chair, looking smug. A moment later Mel appeared in the doorway, carrying Erik on one hip and an enormous bowl of gravy in the other hand.

"Jacquie, you're supposed to be helping set the table."

"I'm keeping Joanne company," Jacquie said virtuously. I gaped at her and Mel laughed out loud.

"I see how it is. All right. You keep Joanne company." She put the gravy down and disappeared back into the kitchen as I yelled, "I'm being used!" after her. Jacquie giggled, pleased with herself, and tilted her chair precariously so she could lean on me. By the time I got her straightened up, the table was set and everyone had gathered around. I lifted my wineglass and my eyebrows, looking to Billy for permission to make a toast.

"To Mel," I said cheerfully. "A miracle of modern efficiency. Thank you for inviting us to dinner." I lifted my glass a little higher, watching the wine catch the bright white of one of the chandelier light-bulbs and turn it red as the full moon. "Oh, *shit!*"

I dropped the wine glass and ran for the door.

CHAPTER 10

I didn't actually get my boots all the way on until Gary had us halfway to the park. I kept fumbling my stupid damned cell phone as I tried to call Morrison. Finally, on the fourth try, I got the right number punched in and he answered with a worn-out hello.

"Morrison? You've got to get everybody out of the park, right now. Do we have anybody there? Call them out. He's going to be there. The Blade. It's the full moon. Mother said the moon was changing. Can you call them out?"

Gary gave me a sideways glance of concern. Billy leaned over the front seat of the cab, hanging on my every word. I had no idea what Mel must think. I hadn't managed to say anything coherent between grabbing my boots and running for the cab.

Apparently I still wasn't saying anything coherent. Morrison was silent on the other end of the line for a few moments, then exhaled heavily. "Walker?"

"Of course it's Walker! Does anybody else do this kind of shit to you? Can you empty the park? They're never going to see him coming, Morrison, they're just going to get killed. You've got to move now!"

Another moment's silence, and then, "I will call you back in two minutes. Do not do anything until you hear back from me." Morrison hung up. I finally pulled my second boot on, wishing my foot weren't soaking wet and cold from melting snow.

"Hurry-hurry-hurry-hurry, Gary, hurry."

"If I hurry any more we'll be dead." It was true. The roads were coated in black ice, and he was driving as fast as I would have, which didn't bode well for anybody.

"Joanie?"

"It's Blade, dammit, it's the full moon." I twitched around to look at Billy, then twitched forward again. "I'm going to have to explain it to Morrison, I don't want to explain it twice." I leaned forward, as if my doing so would urge the cab to a faster pace. "Dammit, dammit, dammit, stupid stupid stupid Jo."

"Hey," Gary said, surprisingly quiet under my litany of abuse. "You got no reason to be callin' yourself stupid, lady."

Unexpected sniffles hit me right in the nose. "No right," I mumbled. "Not no reason."

"Close enough for this old dog."

The cell phone rang and I nearly jumped out of my skin as I answered it. "God, I *hate* these things."

"I assume you're talking about the phone," Morrison said. "The park's clearing out. What the hell is going on, Walker? You'd better not be screwing with me."

"I would not screw with you," I promised fervently. "It's the full moon, Morrison, my mother died on the full moon. It was the solstice, now it's the equinox and the moon is full again. Check the records, I bet that's what it was twenty-seven years ago, too."

"How the hell am I supposed to check the records on the full moon from thirty years ago?"

"There's this really cool Web site," I started, then screwed up my face and grabbed the oh-shit handle as Gary took a corner by use of the Force, without looking where he was going and with no apparent regard to life or limb. "Look, it doesn't matter, I know I'm right. He's killing people on the full moons of winter. This is the last one. Tonight's the equinox. I'm going to stop him."

"How?"

"I have absolutely no idea." I hung up, not wanting to hear Morrison's response to that. To my utter surprise, the phone didn't ring again. Less than two minutes later we pulled into the park's lot. I tumbled out of the cab almost before it stopped moving and ran for the baseball diamond as fast as I could. Gary and Billy came after me, shouting.

I expected to slam into the Blade's red barrier with such force that it'd throw me back. Instead I flung myself at it so hard that I skidded ten feet in the snow when I hit nothing at all. I said something witty and intelligent, like, "Da fuh?" around the mouthful of snow I got for my troubles, and scrambled to my feet, waiting for all hell to break loose.

Somehow, despite everything, I didn't expect it to break loose by way of crimson falling down the face of the moon to cast a bloody shadow on the earth. Everything real seemed to go away: the bite of cold air, the shine of moonlight on fresh snow, my friends' voices yelling somewhere behind me. I stood there with my jaw hanging open, staring up at the bleeding moon, while a sliver fell from it and tumbled all the way to earth.

Just before it hit the ground, it flared a cloak of blackness that cut the air with a banshee scream. Then the cloak settled, the Blade walking forward, tall and thin and hatchet faced. I could feel power rolling off it, heavy as the sea, and with as much concern for the threat I provided as the ocean itself might be.

Right about then it struck me that I was so low on power I'd been punch-drunk and giggling less than an hour earlier, and that out of all the days to pick a fight with something that looked like Morticia Addams's incredibly evil older brother, today might well be the worst possible choice.

The Blade came toward me, faster than a run, without any visible means of locomotion. He simply glided over the blood-colored snow, picking up speed that was all the more eerie for its silence. I did a mental check over my list of available weapons.

There weren't any.

I was going to die.

To my surprise, I discovered I could live with that. I let out the best war cry I could manage—it had nothing on Jacquie's gleeful yelling, but it wasn't bad—and flung myself at the Blade with everything I had.

Which was nothing.

The Blade wasn't prepared for that.

I hit him in the stomach, a shoulder-first tackle Gary would've been proud of. It was like smashing into a flexible block of ice: cold split straight down into my bones and made the marrow into something that carried icy death. He screamed—for the first time I realized the metal-on-metal shriek I'd heard time and again was actually coming from the Blade, a banshee wail straight out of hell.

A banshee wail.

If I'd had time, I'd have stopped to beat my head on

something. I'd called the haunting shrieks *banshee cries* without thinking it through all along. The Blade *was* a banshee. Harbinger of death.

My death, specifically, if I didn't gain the upper hand. We rolled and thumped across the frozen field, struggling for sheer physical dominance. For a moment I had him, but he wrapped bony fingers around my wrist and cold seared into my skin again, numbing my arm all the way to the elbow. I was going to have a dandy case of frostbite if I got out of this alive.

He flung me backward over his head, using my arm like a fulcrum. I actually cartwheeled in the air, watching the blood moon zip by before I smashed into the snow and skidded. I staggered to my feet, turning just in time to catch the Blade's shoulder with my gut, an excellent reversal of my tackle a moment earlier. All the air wheezed out of me and I hit the snow again, doing less skidding and more sinking with his weight on top of me. He was *heavy* for such a skinny thing, as if he'd been emptied of bone and muscle and had cold iron poured into his skin instead. His fingers wrapped around my throat, driving me further into the snow. It felt so warm compared to his hands that for a few seconds I stopped caring, cozy in my snow bed and ready to sleep.

A tiny, offended burst of power flared in my belly, reminding me what real warmth was.

I opened my eyes again, looking up into the Blade's grimacing rictus. I couldn't tell if it had ever been human. Skin stretched across its bones so tightly it might've been a mummy, eyes with bloody fire lighting them staring wide and empty at me. Its teeth—*her* teeth, I finally realized: it was, or had been at one time, female. Of course. Banshees were. *Her* teeth were bared, dry lips pulled back from them.

I wasn't sure she needed to breathe, but her chest was expanding.

Wait. I knew this part. This was where she screamed until my eardrums ruptured. I thought twice in one day was a little much, so I took what warmth the power inside me offered, forced it into my arm, and jabbed upward with two stiffened fingers. Right into her throat.

My fingers went all the way through to her spine with a horrible sound of flesh tearing as easily as paper. The scream turned into an aborted *glerk* and the banshee loosened her hold on me. I kicked her off and rolled away, clapping my hand to my throat, coughing through bruised muscle for air. For a few seconds we stayed there, both swaying, watching each other warily. The hole in her throat sealed up, not like human flesh would, but like paper was being stretched back to fit into a hole it'd been wrinkled away from.

She pounced again and I ducked, absurdly smug at the startled look that brightened her flame-colored eyes as she went flying over my head. Then she tackled me from behind, smashing my face into the snow. I thought, very clearly, *damn, that thing really corners,* and had a brief, irrational moment of wanting to try Petite out against her.

Instead I dragged in a lungful of snow and ice as I shoved so deep into the snow that I hit the earth below it. The banshee's knee was in my back, bearing down with too much weight for me to move. I scrabbled for the worn-out center of power within myself, and came up dry. Apparently I'd blown my one chance when I didn't finish ripping her head off a minute earlier. I pounded a fist in the snow, weak flailing as I tried to buck her off. It was about as effective as threatening to catch a storm in cotton candy.

She bent forward, bony knee pressing into my spine

between my shoulder blades. I thought about screaming, but I couldn't get enough air to. She hissed, right there behind my ear, and I had the horrible idea she was spitting maggots into my hair. Why maggots were a problem when I was about to be dead, I didn't know, but the idea completely grossed me out. "In the womb I heard you die, for no one lives when a banshee cries."

I wasn't just going to die. I was going to be rhymed to death. That simply wasn't fair. I flailed again, wishing my arms didn't feel so heavy. Wishing my legs would kick, instead of lying there getting colder. Wishing I could wake up enough energy inside me to reach out for more. I didn't even have enough to ask the city to hit me with its best shot, a tactic I'd tried once before and had sworn I wouldn't do again. That I even thought about trying told me I was in dire straits.

"The pregnant gwyld was clever and wise, took you away from prying eyes. Should have known it couldn't last, power like yours can't be passed." Her voice was singsong and scaly, grating against the ringing in my ears. I tried jerking my head back. Not even a banshee could like a head butt to the bridge of the nose, right? But the weight of her hand was too much to move. I considered giving up and dying. It was pretty clearly in the books. On the other hand, she was saying something interesting, if I could get enough oxygen to my brain to work my way through her bad poetry. "Master sees and Master hears, gains his strength through blood-red tears. Thirty years he's gone unfed, shaman's gifts protect the dead."

The words burrowed into my brain, extracting details about my life in exchange for my fumbling grasp of what the banshee was telling me. I whimpered into the snow and tried hard to hang on to the idea of my name wrapped safely up in airbags and seat belts. I felt the scrape of her voice slide off that thought, and nearly laughed with relief. I could keep her away from the most important things. At least if I was going to die, I wasn't going to die with my soul eaten.

Power erupted in my belly like molten gold being poured into me. I straightened my arms, suddenly filled with strength, and shoved up, lifting the Blade's weight as if it were inconsequential. I whipped around, flinging her off me, and she landed yards away, skidding through the snow on hands and knees, back arched like an angry cat. For an instant, the banshee cries stopped, leaving a silence so profound it hurt me in my bones.

I had no time to wonder where the new strength was coming from. I drew on the memory of my mother, throwing up a jail cell made of her own will, and copied it. Bars of blazing silver flashed up out of the snow, slamming closed around the banshee. She threw her head back and keened, a high piercing note that shivered all the way to the bloody moon. My bars wavered under the onslaught, and her voice strengthened, the moon itself seeming to hang lower in the sky the longer she wailed.

Black threads of power, the sacrificed lives of three women, wound together and responded to the banshee's cries. They leaped through the bars I'd built, piercing her bony body. She grew in size and in power, feeding from the blood lines, which throbbed and pulsed like arteries as they spread across the snow. I dug deeper into the fresh power I'd found, discovering an ocean's depth of energy waiting to be tapped. It ran deeper than I did, the same kind of power that Billy had tapped into earlier that day. The love of family, the protective streak that went beyond what a single person could encompass. I could use it, but I doubted I'd live through it.

It didn't matter.

The ocean of blue crushed down upon the banshee, pressing down to sever the blood lines. They flattened, carrying less sustenance but refusing to shatter. I felt half-moon cuts opening up on my palms, my hands fisted so tightly that blood couldn't escape the tiny slices my fingernails made. The banshee kept screaming, her voice muffled by the weight of my power, but not yet broken. I set my teeth together and reached deeper into the core of power I'd tapped, willing to die as long as I took the other bitch with me.

Sheila MacNamarra put her hand in mine, pale and wraithlike in the bloody moonlight. There was no substance to her, only a terrible force of will, and with her touch a heart of coldness broke inside me. I gave her one shocked look and she returned it with a smile as warm as the summer sun.

"We started this nearly thirty years ago, now didn't we?" The lilt in her voice turned thirty into *tarty*. "Let's put an end to it, shall we?"

That morning, and almost thirty years ago, I'd thrown her a fastball of my own power. Now she made good on the gift, returning it threefold. The depth I'd reached, the unexpected strength, wasn't mine at all, and it wouldn't, in the end, tap me out. It was my mother who would die for it. My mother who had already died for it.

Golden strength and red temper flowed into me, blending with my own silvers and blues in a way I hadn't seen before. She shored up the silver bars of the cage I'd built, added her weight to that of the deep blue sea. Out of the corner of my eye I saw her nod, and found myself walking forward, my fingers trailing in the golden depth of her strength.

I slipped between the bars of the cage I'd built, putting my hand all the way into Sheila's power, and withdrawing a sword made of fire. I recognized the shape of it: a rapier with a sweeping guard that flickered and warmed my hand without burning me. Flames shimmered to a deadly edge along the slender blade. The Banshee's screams erupted all over again, but the power bearing down on her muffled them and left my beleaguered ears in no real danger.

The black lines of blood magic that fed her parted under the sword's blade where they'd refused to disintegrate under raw force. *A scalpel*, I thought. *My mother was a scalpel. And I came so close to never knowing that. To not understanding.*

The banshee stopped screaming when the lines were cut, her gaze fixed on the red moon, as if waiting for rescue to come. I glanced up at it, then shook my head. "He's still locked behind bars." Not bars. Behind a fallen cave mouth, the broken stones held in place by my mother's will. My mother, who, with my help, had disrupted the sacrifice that would feed him, almost thirty years ago. And with her help I'd done it again tonight. "Still hungry, too." I leaned in, my hands shaking. "Too weak to help you, bitch."

Surprise creased the Blade's narrow face as I took her head, the fiery rapier ripping through her neck with the sound of paper tearing, loud in the absence of her cries. I caught her falling head with a grace that bewildered me, fingers knotted in her thin hair, and walked away from the dusty bones with a spot of emptiness building inside me. All the power that had been brought to bear, both mine and the dark stuff birthed by the banshee's murders, faded, clear moonlight reestablishing itself over the frozen fields.

My mother, wearing the cable-knit sweater and jeans she'd worn in her youth, folded her arms beneath her breasts and smiled at me.

"Mom..." I hadn't ever called her that before. It made my throat tight, and her smile fragile. "You brought me to America to protect me from that thing, didn't you?" The banshee's rhymes finally made sense. "So it couldn't find me."

Her smile flickered, still fragile, and she lifted her chin. I saw, quite clearly, the silver Celtic cross of a necklace that rested against her collarbone, momentarily exposed by the shift of her sweater. I pressed my fingers against my throat, where the same necklace now rested.

"I thought it was for the best, lass. You told me, you see. Before you were born, you told me I hadn't succeeded in destroying the Blade. It was all I could think of to do, to protect you."

I closed my eyes briefly, remembering the way joy had bled from her expression and left resolution in its place. I nodded in a jerky motion, and made myself open my eyes again. "Thank you."

"I thought I could explain when you were grown. When you came to see me. But you weren't ready." Grief colored the shadow of her smile. "So closed off, Siobhán. Whatever happened to you, that turned you away from the wonders of the world?" She lifted her hand, staying my answer before I had a chance to give it. "There's no time, not anymore. There hasn't been since the beginning. Bitter ashes, isn't it, but that's the price of Gaelic blood, my Siobhán. For all their wars are merry."

"And all their songs are sad," I whispered. Surprise brought out her smile and let it fade into pleasure at my recognition of the quote.

"It was all I could think of to do, loose myself from the world. I could see it in you, Siobhán. Joanne. My Joanne. That the moment was coming when you'd have to choose. I thought if I could hold on in spirit, I might protect you for a little while. Distract the darker things while you grew to understand your gifts."

"You did." My throat was still tight. I tried swallowing against it, but came up dry. "You were here. I would have died tonight. Thank you. I...will I see you again?" She was fading around the edges now, like the Cheshire Cat. I knew the answer even before she shook her head, and looked away to hide the shock of loneliness I felt stab through me.

"The space of the winter moons was all I could bargain for. I was afraid even it might not be enough."

"Bargain?" I looked back at her, what was left to see. She looked younger somehow, the smile that curved her mouth belonging to a woman I'd hardly known.

"Goodbye, Siobhán. Know that I love you." There was nothing left but her smile, and then even that was gone.

MORRISON HAD JOINED BILLY and Gary at the bleachers when I walked back to them. None of them seemed to see me coming. Gary clutched his chest and sat down with a thud, glaring at me as I clumped up to the bleachers. "What the hell happened out there, Jo?"

"What'd you see?"

"Not a goddamned thing! You ran off and now you're back!"

I looked up at the sky. The moon seemed higher than it had been, more solid and real somehow. "It didn't seem that long to me."

Morrison was staring grimly at the head I still carried. "Is that the killer?"

I lifted the head a few inches. "Yeah."

"Where's the rest of it?"

"Out there." I turned around, waving the banshee's head at the field.

There was no body lying in the snow, nor any sign of the wrestling fight I'd had with her. The only footprints at all in the new snow were mine, leading up to the bleachers. Even they only seemed to begin a few yards away, just on this side of the closest blood line that had been drawn with one of the victim's entrails. I stood there a few seconds, waiting for a clever explanation to pop into mind.

Nothing did. After a moment I looked at the head again, then over my shoulder at Morrison as I hefted it. "Do you want me to bring this in?"

It took a long time for him to say no. I nodded and gave it a swing or two, then threw it back the way I came. It arched and hit the snow with a soft poof, powder flying in the air. When it cleared, there was no mark that suggested anything had landed on the smooth white surface.

"It's over," Morrison said, almost a question. I nodded. Billy let out a whistle that split the air and shoved his hands in his pockets with an air of finality.

"So who wants to come back to the house for dinner? I bet Mel kept it warm. Why don't you come with us, Captain? There's plenty."

Gary stomped down the bleachers, Billy a step or two behind him. Morrison looked at me. I kept my head turned a little to the side, meeting his eyes. He finally nodded and jerked his chin. "Let's go."

Tension ebbed from my shoulders and I dropped my

chin to my chest. "Captain." Not Morrison. I didn't know why.

Morrison turned, eyebrows lifted. I swallowed, trying to figure out the right thing to say. Neither "thank you" nor "sorry" seemed exactly appropriate. I stood there gazing at him until he developed a faint, surprisingly understanding smile. "Come on, Walker," he said, more gently. "We're done here." He tilted his head again and walked down the bleachers after the other two.

I let out a deep breath and followed them all, smiling at the moon.

Acknowledgments

I'm delighted to be republishing *Banshee Cries* as an elevated-to-full-book-status in the Walker Papers, and would like to tip my hat to G&S Cover Design Studio for the glorious new cover art!

I'd also like to thank the original editor for this project, Mary-Theresa Hussey, for commissioning it: it's been a pleasure watching this little book do its job all these years, and it literally wouldn't exist without her.

And lastly, of course, but obviously not leastly, all my love is due to Dad, and Ted, and Henry!

-Catie

About the Author

CE Murphy began writing around age six, when she submitted three poems to a school publication. The teacher producing the magazine selected (inevitably) the one she thought was by far the worst, but also told her–a six year old kid–to keep writing, which she has.

She has also held the usual grab-bag of jobs usually seen in an authorial biography, including public library volunteer (at ages 9 and 10; it's clear she was doomed to a career involving books), archival assistant, cannery worker, and web designer. Writing books is better.

She was born and raised in Alaska, and now lives with her family in her ancestral homeland of Ireland.

You can most reliably find her online at catiemurphy.com.